René looked beautiful. She moved fluidly about the kitchen in that sexy sundress. It swayed and folded around her hips, and before Jon knew it he'd lost control of his tongue.

"You know what my favorite part of the birthing class was?"

His relationship with René had taken a new direction over the last three weeks. He hadn't set out to let this intimate shift happen, but it had, and he didn't have a clue how to deal with it.

But he couldn't shut off the quiet roar of desire building even now, and for the first time he dropped the shield and didn't bother to stop himself.

He moved toward her and, from behind, placed his hands lightly on her arms.

"Getting to put my hands on you." His voice, heavy with the last threads of restraint, almost cracked when he whispered over her ear. He slid his hands over her baby mound and wondered at the warmth and roundness.

He was about to spin her around when she moved voluntarily toward his body. Her arms wrapped around his back and she nuzzled her cheek against his chest, the feel of her arms drawing him in.

They were this odd couple, family-to-be—a choice they'd made based on her wish.

And their future?

He stroked the thick layers of her hair. She lifted her chin and he claimed her mouth with a breath of a kiss. Tender. Gentle. Warm.

Lynne Marshall has been a Registered Nurse in a large California hospital for twenty-five years. She has now taken the leap to writing full-time, but still volunteers at her local community hospital. After writing the book of her heart in 2000, she discovered the wonderful world of Medical™ Romance, where she feels the freedom to write the stories she loves. She is happily married, has two fantastic grown children, and a socially challenged rescue dog. Besides her passion for writing Medical™ Romance, she loves to travel and read. Thanks to the family dog, she takes long walks every day! To find out more about Lynne, please visit her website: www.lynnemarshallweb.com

Recent titles by the same author:

THE BOSS AND NURSE ALBRIGHT
TEMPORARY DOCTOR, SURPRISE FATHER

THE
HEART DOCTOR
AND THE BABY

BY
LYNNE MARSHALL

First published in Great Britain 2010
Large Print edition 2011
Harlequin Mills & Boon Limited,
Eton House, 18-24 Paradise Road,
Richmond, Surrey TW9 1SR

© Janet Maarschalk 2010

ISBN: 978 0 263 21719 3

Harlequin Mills & Boon policy is to use papers that are natural, renewable and recyclable products and made from wood grown in sustainable forests. The logging and manufacturing process conform to the legal environmental regulations of the country of origin.

Printed and bound in Great Britain
by CPI Antony Rowe, Chippenham, Wiltshire

For my mother, Lura,
for teaching me unconditional
and abiding love.

CHAPTER ONE

RENÉ MUNROE hadn't been this nervous since her first date at fifteen. Today, twenty years later, she worked like a madwoman to prepare a meal for her coworker, Jon Becker.

She used whole tomatoes and garlic cloves, fresh basil and, because she liked tangy instead of sweet, she added her signature dash of balsamic vinegar to the marinara sauce. Then she went the extra mile to make the pasta from scratch.

Tonight, if she handled things perfectly, could turn out to be an "extra mile" kind of night. The linguini looked delicious as she pulled the noodles through the gizmo, hoping all would turn out as planned. Add a salad of baby greens and fresh Italian bread from her favorite bakery, and she had a meal. A darn fine meal. A meal that might lead to a dream come true.

She brushed off her hands, grabbed the dishes

and tableware and hipped her way through the swinging kitchen door to the dining room while trying to push nervous thoughts out of her mind. Could she pull this off? She distracted herself by setting the table.

Three years ago she'd found a classic Craftsman home in disrepair in the foothills of Santa Barbara. Since it was close enough to the medical clinic, she bought it for a good price and little by little began restoring it. The dining and living rooms were her favorite parts of the house. She'd knocked out one wall to bring an open, flowing feel to the area, but had maintained and refinished all of the built-in shelves and extra woodwork. This was a home she intended to live in for the rest of her life. A home she hoped to have a family in.

She believed in keeping design uncluttered, like her life, and the simple dining table and chairs with a matching buffet were the only furniture in this room. Sage-green walls brought peace to her roiling jitters, and were a perfect contrast to the abundant rich golden wood.

After tonight, if all went well, the last thing her life would be was simple.

She put bright red place mats on the table to contrast the subtle earthenware vase heavily laden with colorful dried flowers. She needed things to be just so tonight, and did a quick walk-through of the living room to make sure nothing was out of place.

A natural-rock fireplace served as the focal point, and even though she'd cheated with a gas log, the fire gave the living room that extra bit of coziness she wanted. Anything to help make easier the topic she was about to bring up with Jon.

One mad dash to the bathroom to touch up her makeup and run the comb through her hair, and she was ready…just as the doorbell rang. Perfect timing.

Jon stood on her porch with his typical serious expression and a bottle of wine in each hand. Along with his usual salt-and-pepper-brown closely cropped hair, he sported a new beard tracing a thin red-tinged line along his jaw, and wore a black fleece vest, long-sleeved gray shirt and jeans. When she let him in, he smelled good, like sandalwood and some exotic spice, and it struck her that she'd never noticed his cologne before.

"Wow," he said. "You've really done a lot with the house. It looks great."

He'd helped her do a walk-through when she'd first considered buying it, and had given his nod of approval. After his divorce two years ago, she wasn't sure how to handle their mostly business relationship and, not wanting to send the wrong message, hadn't invited him back again. He'd struck her as a recluse since then, avoiding anything that smacked of social interaction. In fact, she'd been pleasantly surprised when he'd accepted without protest her invitation for dinner.

Had it really been that long since he'd been here? She thanked him and gestured for him to sit while she opened the wine, but instead he followed her into the kitchen.

"I thought I was the high-tech guy," he said, "but look at you, going all stainless steel."

"Yeah, I upgraded," she said with a laugh as she popped the cork out of the bottle, splashed some wine into the glasses and walked him back to the living room. Small talk had never been a problem with Jon, but they'd never ventured deeper than that, and definitely had never come close to what she needed to discuss with him tonight.

"We should probably let the wine breathe," she said, wishing she could catch her breath, too. The moment she'd seen Jon her heart started tapping out odd beats, and right this minute it felt as if someone was juggling in her stomach. What she was about to ask him was the craziest idea she'd ever had in her entire life.

"Dinner smells fantastic," he said.

"I hope you're hungry." She did her best to appear nonchalant, as if her future didn't depend on the outcome of tonight's meal. "Let's sit for a bit, and…uh, talk. I've got some cheese and crackers to go with the wine."

Long and lean, Jon settled into the hardy wood-and-earth-tone upholstered chair that went so well with the style of the house. Come to think of it, he looked as if he belonged there. She sat in its mate so they could both share the small table where she'd already laid out the appetizers. He tossed a couple of crackers topped with the nutty cheese-ball spread into his mouth before he sampled the wine.

When was the appropriate time to bring up the subject? Surely there wasn't any etiquette for when to broach the topic of artificial insemination amongst friends. She took a long swig of the wine and felt her mouth dry up. "I need some water—can I get you any?"

By now, with her uneasy behavior, he'd gotten that suspicious glint in his eyes, the one she'd often seen him give a patient fudging about their diet or medicine. She'd been way too skittish, and Jon could tell something was up.

"You seem really anxious." His eyes brightened. "Is it me?" He snapped his fingers. "It's the beard, isn't it?"

She swiped the air. "Gosh, no. Jon! The beard?" If she'd given it any thought at all, she'd admit the beard complemented his carved features, but beards were the last thing on her mind tonight. She took another sip of wine, then headed straight to the kitchen to gather her thoughts, soon emerging with ice water for both of them.

He waited with a thoughtful expression, brows

faintly furrowed. "The beard was my daughters' idea." He scratched the triangular swatch beneath his lower lip, and straightened in his chair as if uncomfortable with the added masculinity.

"It's a nice addition. Really." Why did she need to say "really" if she'd meant it in the first place? Oh, if only her jitters would go away she might act like the normal person he knew from the clinic, instead of a nervous, stammering mental job.

He grew serious and shifted on the cushion, as if his curiosity had reached its apex. "There's a reason besides eating dinner that made you invite me tonight, isn't there?" His narrowed, probing stare made her spine straighten. "And I'm fairly sure it isn't to talk about my facial hair."

She needed another glass of wine and quick. "There *is* something I'd like to talk about, Jon." Oh, God, how was she going to do this? "But let's do it over dinner, okay?"

"Oh-kay." If he had an inquisitive look before, now he bore the expression of a sleuth about to solve the crime of the century.

She stood and he followed her to the table.

She couldn't stand still and made a dash for the kitchen.

"Can I help with anything?" he asked through the door.

"Just sit. I'll be right back."

Thankful for the distraction, she swept through the kitchen, put the pasta on to boil, flung open the refrigerator for the salads and, gathering up the basket of bread before hitting the door, delivered the icy cold plates, dressing and bread all in one swoop.

The two of them became miserably bad at small talk as they ate, especially since she'd hinted at a much bigger topic. He glanced at her and her gaze flitted away, suddenly finding the bread of interest. She snuck another look at him; he chased a grape tomato around his plate. The mounting awkwardness made her grateful when the pasta timer went off and she rushed back into the kitchen to serve up the main course.

Jon tore the bread apart and dipped it into the sauce. "This is great, just great," he said after his first taste.

"I'm glad you like it." Normally she loved to

watch a man enjoy his meal, but this time around all she could do was nod and smile, and try not to break out into welts over what she was about to bring up.

Deep breath. Swallow.

"So the thing is…Jon… I was, uh, wondering…" She nibbled on bread and twirled her fork around in the noodles, over and over again, no appetite whatsoever.

Jon leaned against the slated straight-back chair. She saw the wheels turning and the cogs meshing in his genius-level mind and knew she couldn't stall another second.

"You know you're driving me nuts, right?" he said, planting his fork into his pasta.

She closed her eyes and blurted. "What's your take on artificial insemination?"

His fork stopped midbite. He shut his mouth and dropped a look on her that said she'd potentially lost her mind, every last bit of it. "In general? Or for some specific reason?"

She swallowed what felt like a paper towel, a large and grainy paper towel. "Let's start with… in general."

"For someone who has fertility issues or no partner..." He began in his typical professorial manner, then narrowed one eye. "Is this pertaining to you?" he asked, an incredulous gaze on his face.

It was indeed pertaining to her and now was the time to get serious. No more skirting the issue. This tack was making her come off foolish and flaky, and on the topic of artificial insemination, she was anything but.

She'd done her homework, had read with interest about the local donor bank, no doubt supplied by multiple university students in need of extra cash. Wondered if she could go through with choosing an anonymous donor based on her list of specific requirements and qualities. Though it would serve her purpose, twenty-first century or not, how cold was that? Images of immature, beer-goggled university boys flashed through her mind, and a firm twist in her gut had kept her from logging into the Web site. Then she'd thought about her list of requirements and one particular face had popped into her mind.

She finished off the last few sips of wine and

carefully placed the glass on the table. "I'm seriously considering it, Jon. I'm not getting any younger, and I don't see Mr. Right walking in my front door anytime in the near future." She grabbed his hand, didn't realize she'd done it until she felt his hard knuckles and lean fingers. She'd never touched him in this needful way before. "I want a baby, more than you can imagine."

"And you want my opinion about this because…?" It was his turn to guzzle the wine.

Her eyes couldn't stretch any wider. Since she'd finally opened up the topic, she decided to go all the way. "Traditionally, my wanting a baby would entail finding the right guy, getting married and settling down." She blurted her thoughts as her eyes roamed around and around the room. "Unless some miracle occurs in the near future, marriage and pregnancy isn't going to happen. But this is the twenty-first century, who says I have to be traditional?"

His suspicious look, along with the expression of terror, almost made her laugh as she went for the grand finale. How *did* one go about asking a man for his DNA? She grimaced. Very carefully.

"And I brought the topic up with you, because in my opinion…you'd be the perfect donor."

He choked, bobbled his glass, which toppled over and spilled. They both jumped up to mop up the liquid.

"I'm sorry," he said.

"Oh, no, it was my fault for dropping a bomb on you."

He strode into the kitchen and reappeared with a towel, then when he'd absorbed the last of the wine with it, he produced a damp sponge to clean the wood. "I hope this doesn't stain."

"It's the least of my worries." She fought with several strands of hair that had fallen in her face during the fuss over the table.

He went still as the topic noticeably sunk in. "Wow. You're really serious about this."

She met his gaze and gave an assertive nod.

He scraped his jaw, and paced the dining room. "Wow."

"Will you at least think about it?"

"Wow." The bona fide genius, Jon Becker, had melted down to uttering a single-syllable echo.

She'd finally gathered her wits and was ready to talk business. "I've jotted down some thoughts about everything, and maybe you can give me your input—" oh, what an unfortunate choice of words "—about anything I may have overlooked?"

His dark eyes took on the wariness of a wild animal. He seemed to need to hold his jaw shut with his hand. After a few seconds considering her proposition, he dropped another look on her that made her take a breath. "You want me to be a father again at forty-two?"

She thought carefully how to best respond. "No, Jon. I want you to donate your sperm so I can be a mother at thirty-six."

He went perfectly still, stared at her as if he'd never seen her before. "You want a designer baby?"

Sudden calm enveloped her, and clarity of thought finally followed. "Let's sit down." She gestured toward the living room to the small sofa in front of the fireplace. He followed.

"I've already got my daughters, I don't want any more kids," he said. "And I'm planning a sabbatical once Lacy graduates and goes off to college. I've waited a long time to be free again."

"You won't have to be a part of the baby's life. I'm just asking you to be the sperm donor."

"Why not ask Phil? He's single. Young."

"He's also a playboy and irresponsible." She left out the part that she preferred Jon's nose to Phil's. "Jon, I've thought about everyone I know, and you are the top of the list. You're intelligent, healthy… you have an endearing personality—" How was she supposed to tell him the next part? She took a deep breath and spit it out. "And I think your DNA would work really well with mine."

"A superbaby?"

"A baby. Just a baby with a lot going for it. I'll take complete responsibility for the child. Nothing—I repeat, nothing—will be expected of you beyond your, uh—" her eyes fluttered and she suddenly needed to swallow "—donation." She tugged her earlobe and hoped she wasn't blushing, though her face definitely heated up.

"All things considered, your job will be relatively easy."

Their eyes met and he seemed hesitant, as if he'd mentally walked his way through exactly what his part would be, and was completely uncomfortable with her proposition.

"But we work together," he said. "How on earth am I supposed to not be involved?"

"I admit it could get tricky, but if you just put yourself in a clinical frame of mind, think of it as a scientific experiment between friends and colleagues, it could work."

He didn't look convinced.

She patted his hand, the same hand she'd never touched before tonight. "I just know we can handle this."

He didn't look nearly as sure as she professed to be, but she homed in to the subtle willingness to explore the possibilities with him, and seized her opportunity.

An hour or two or three later, after they'd discussed everything from health history to parental obligations or, in his case, lack thereof, to attorney input and whether or not to do home insemination versus clinical, intravaginal or intracervical insemination, the bizarre nature of their conversation seemed almost normal, as if two medical colleagues were discussing lab results.

"You feel like some dessert?" she asked.

He laughed, but admitted he did.

Amazingly, he ate every bite of the apple-and-berry torte she'd picked up at the bakery. Then, when it was time to leave, he hesitated. "I need time to think this over, René."

"Of course! I'm just grateful you haven't gone bolting out my door, peeling tire rubber trying to get away."

"I wouldn't run out on you." He squeezed her shoulder.

"I know that, Jon." She ducked her head against his chest, something else she'd never done with him before tonight, then quickly lifted it.

"I guess I'd better be going." It was almost midnight.

"When you make your decision, if it's yes, all you have to do is give me the nod and I'll have my attorney draw up a contract. If you do decide to help me with this, I won't hold you responsible in any way, Jon. You have my word. I promise."

He took a breath and got a goofy look on his face. "In that case, we could save all kinds of trouble and do this the old-fashioned way," he said with a devilish glint in his eyes.

An absurd laugh escaped her lips, and she socked his arm. Jon thought more like most men than she'd imagined. "You're such a joker." Though in the five years she'd known him, *joker* was never a word she'd use to describe him.

They'd had a conversation about creating a life without sex. He'd recited the statistics on success rates depending on his motility, and her fertility considering her age. They'd taken it to the scientific level, which made sense since they were both doctors, and he'd almost agreed to the plan. She wasn't about to throw one major potentially mind-blowing wrench into the mix, no matter what he suggested in jest. The old-fashioned way? No way. No how.

She bit her lip and stared at him. As their gazes fused, a new understanding bridged between them. Under the most unlikely circumstances, they'd taken their business relationship to a new level. Whether Jon decided to take her up on the deal or not, things between them would never be the same.

Jon could run a hundred miles and still not work out the crazy mix of emotions sluicing through him. He'd woken up early—hell, he'd never officially fallen asleep by true sleep study standards—and after tossing and turning he'd gotten up before sunrise and hit the Santa Barbara foothills. What little REM time he did manage had been cluttered with vivid dreams about babies and doctor babes, outlandish propositions and some interesting positions, too. At one point, René had straddled him. He liked that part of his dream, yet it had made him sit bolt upright, disoriented. And poof, the sexy vision had vanished.

A sudden steep hill forced him back into the moment, and he hit it with determination, refusing to slow his pace. Last night, in another transition from non-REM to early REM, he'd seen René as if looking through the wrong end of a telescope, motioning to him to follow her as she floated farther and farther away toward a baby. A tiny baby. In a test tube.

Crazy dreams matched by crazy thoughts.

His lungs burned with each stride, his leg muscles protested with aches and near cramps, but he refused to stop, refused to give in to the hill. That damn proposition. He had plans, for crying out loud! He was going to take a sabbatical and travel to the Far East. He'd study with Asian healers and cardiologists and learn their methods while imparting his knowledge. His daughters had reached the age where they'd be going out into the world, and he dreamed about doing the same. Finally!

It still seemed unreal that two years ago his wife, out of the blue, had asked for a divorce after seventeen years of marriage. It had sent him reeling in disbelief; even now the thought released a thousand icy needles in his chest. What had he done wrong? How had she fallen out of love with him? If he couldn't trust her to keep her word in marriage, what woman on this planet could he ever trust?

He'd withdrawn and lived the life of a recluse since then, even going so far as to take up long-distance running, anything to avoid other people. His medical practice and plans for a sabbatical had kept him going when he didn't think he could go on. That and his relationship with his daughters.

René had asked him to consider this "deed" a special gift to her, and that he wouldn't be involved beyond the initial donation. He could tell by the solidly sincere look in her eyes that she wanted a chance to have a baby, but would it be a passing whim?

And more importantly, based on his experience with his ex-wife, could he trust that giving his sperm would be the extent of his involvement with René?

That afternoon, the MidCoast Medical staff meeting dragged on. René stealthily tapped her foot under the table and listened to Jason recite the quarterly reports.

Her mind wandered, dying to know if Jon had made his decision yet, but doing her best not to make eye contact with him. She didn't want to pressure him.

"We've balanced our budget, which means we'll be able to buy that new lab equipment we've been wanting," Jason said, using a laser pen to highlight the slide behind him. "And if things keep up this way, in a few more months we won't have to send our patients to the local hospital for bronchoscopies. We can do them here."

"That would be fantastic," Phil Hansen said. "I've been waiting a long time for that."

The clinic, housed in a renovated Victorian mansion in downtown Santa Barbara, was thriving. The four-doctor practice had taken a risk and prevailed against the odds. They'd built a clientele from nothing and reached out to the community, and their hard work had finally paid off.

Jason gave his signature broad smile—the one he'd been wearing ever since he'd fallen in love with and married Claire, the nurse practitioner. "Who'd have thought that five years ago when we conceived the idea to join forces and build our own clinic, we'd come this far?" he said, glancing toward his partners, then at his pregnant wife.

"Me," Jon raised his hand. "We did our homework, studied the demographics, discovered the perfect location and need for the clinic. We had your money, Jason," Jon added with a smirk, "and business expertise. We were bound to succeed."

He analyzed everything and, genius that he was, always did a fine job. René glanced fondly into his luminous brown eyes, which softened ever so slightly when their gazes met. She nodded and smiled. He smiled back—a masculine take on Mona Lisa. The kind of understated yet proud smile that made René react in her gut whether she wanted to or not.

Was he sending a subtle message? Had he made his decision?

Claire shifted in her chair, her brows knotted together and lips slightly pursed. René had seen that same look hundreds of times on the faces of her third trimester patients. Toward the end of the pregnancy, constantly searching for comfort, all they longed for was to get that baby out of there! René offered a smile of encouragement as she locked gazes with her newest friend in the medical group.

Claire attempted to smile back, then tossed

a glance toward the ceiling as if searching for moral support. Though considered a high-risk pregnancy since Claire also had lupus, René had seen her patient through nothing but smooth sailing from the first day she'd examined her.

Claire was expecting her second child—Jason and Claire's first together—and their newfound love was nothing short of a miracle. It gave René hope that anything was possible. Even for her.

As René listened to the rest of Jason's report, she stared at her lap, at the hands that had delivered countless babies…and the noticeably empty ring finger. Her thirty-sixth birthday was next month and this year, for the first time in her life, she'd become aware of distant keening. That ticking biological clock had never bothered her before, but now consumed her thoughts, drove her crazy with the desire to be a mother. Even to the point of making a fool of herself by asking Jon to be a sperm donor. Rather than cringe, she glanced longingly at Claire's very pregnant state.

Claire gasped.

René went on alert. "Are you all right?"

"Fine," Claire said, releasing the word with a cleansing breath. "Been having Braxton Hicks all day."

René quirked a brow. "All day? Why didn't you say something?"

Claire shrugged. "Second-kid syndrome?"

Since Claire wasn't due for another few weeks, she'd keep her eye on her as the meeting continued.

Phil shot up, forcing her to crane her neck toward the ceiling. His longish dark blond hair swept back from his face in a cavalier manner. Tanned and too handsome for his own good, he read his obligatory monthly OSHA report, and tortured them with rules running the gamut from what chemicals were acceptable to how to dispose of soiled dressings. She prayed the pulmonary faction of their group wouldn't tell them it was time for another disaster drill. And if he did, how soon could she schedule a vacation?

Claire let out another gasp, this time grabbing her back. René checked her watch. It had only been one minute since the last one.

CHAPTER TWO

JASON flew to his wife's side, the one she was holding with both hands. "Sweetheart, is there anything I can do?"

Claire diligently practiced her birthing breathing as René knelt in front of her. She put her palm on Claire's rigid stomach. The baby had dropped from yesterday's appointment and, from the feel of the rock-solid mound, was already engaged.

"I have an idea," René said. "Why don't we adjourn this meeting, and I'll take you to my office and examine you?"

"No argument from me," Claire said.

The confirmed bachelor of the group, Phil, had noticeably paled beneath his Santa Barbara tan. "I guess I'll take off, then," he said, looking relieved.

Jason gingerly assisted his wife to stand, and escorted her, like the deliciously doting soon-to-be father he was, to René's examination room in the clinic.

Jon stood perfectly still, obvious wheels turning in that wondrous mind of his. He glanced at René. "You need any help?"

"Don't know yet," she said, as she rushed out of the kitchen-turned-conference room. "Why don't you stick around just in case?"

Five minutes later, René placed Claire's feet in the stirrups on the table, gowned up and donned gloves, then started the examination. Holy smokes! Not only was she almost effaced and dilated, but her waters had broken.

"We're having a baby here," René called over her shoulder, which had Jason rushing into the room.

"That's what I was afraid of," Claire said, worry knitting her brows.

"Do we have time to get her to the hospital?" Jason asked, sounding breathless.

"Not at this stage." René gave Jason an assertive glance, then she saw Claire's questioning expression. "Don't worry, Claire. I'm here. I'll take care of you."

"Ask Mrs. Densmore if she can keep Gina tonight," Claire said to Jason.

He stood at Claire's side, eyes dilated and wider than René had ever seen them. "Everything's going to be fine," he said, squeezing his wife's fingers with one hand, fishing out his cell phone and speed-dialing their babysitter with the other.

From outside the door, she heard Jon's voice. "How can I help?"

"Get a case of the absorbent towels, and warm some baby bath blankets, then start an IV for me," she said.

A familiar-sounding scream tore from Claire's chest. "Jason, get our morphine supply and an antiemetic. It might help Claire take the edge off before she goes into transition." René waited for the contraction to diminish, then positioned the fetoscope to get an initial heart rate. She delivered babies at the local hospital, not in their clinic, and electronic fetal monitoring wasn't available here.

"Oh, and call for standby ambulance transportation," she added. After the birth, both mother and child would need to be admitted to the local hospital for observation. René bent her head and concentrated on timing the strong and steady beats. *One hundred and thirty beats a minute. Good.*

René stared into Claire's stressed-out green eyes, sending her calming thoughts. Only thirty seconds later another contraction mounted, and perspiration formed around Claire's honey-colored hairline. René continued listening for abnormal deceleration of the baby's heart rate with the contraction, and was relieved to find a normal variation. Only a ten-beat dip.

Jason lurched back into the room with the IV supplies, and when his hands proved too shaky to stick his own wife, Jon stepped in and started the IV as Jason titrated a tiny amount of morphine into the line to help ease Claire's pain in between the contractions. She didn't want Claire too relaxed when it came time to push; the baby could come out floppy instead of vigorously crying.

The labor went on for another hour and a half, when René felt the rigid beginnings of a massive contraction. Now fully effaced and dilated, Claire had moved into transition.

"Push," René said.

Though Claire seemed exhausted, she gave her all. This time the head fully crowned. When the next contraction rode in on the tail end of the first, René continued her encouragement. "Use the contraction, Claire," René said. "Push!"

Jon hovered at René's side. "I'll get a basin for the afterbirth," he said. "Are you going to need to do an episiotomy?"

"Don't think so, but get a small surgical kit for me just in case." She intended to do her part to slow down the passage of the head to avoid any tissue tear.

Jon dashed out of the room as if he were the expectant father, and when he returned, René put him to work tracking the baby's heart rate through the fetoscope so she could concentrate on the birth. Not only was he fascinated with the listening device—typical of him—he was most likely figuring out a way to make a better one.

All was well, but the contractions came so quickly and hard that Claire didn't have time to relax in between. Wringing with sweat, she looked exhausted, ready to give up. Along came another contraction.

"Bear down, Claire! Push! Push!" René urged, as she cupped the baby's head in her hands and moved it downward as Claire pushed with everything she had. Her legs trembled and she let fly words René hadn't heard since the last Lakers basketball game she'd attended.

She slipped the umbilical cord free of the baby's face, and assisted as first the head, then one shoulder and then the other, slipped out. No sooner had the mouth cleared the birth canal, than the baby cried.

Obviously relieved after delivering the hardest part—the head—Claire wept.

René glanced up long enough to see tears fill Jason's eyes. "Oh, my God," he said. The room went blurry for her, too, but she couldn't dwell on the swell of emotion taking over; she had a baby to finish delivering.

The baby slipped out, and René skillfully caught him, as she'd done so many times over her career, but this one felt more special than all the rest. It was her partner and friend's baby. This infant sent her dreaming of birthing her own baby, of daring to hope she'd get the chance.

"It's a beautiful boy," she said, wiping the baby's mouth and face with the warm and soft blanket that her new assistant, Jon, had handed her. He gave her another. After a quick check of the perfect little body, she wrapped the baby up as if the most precious thing in the world, and Jon produced a syringe bulb to suction the baby's mouth and nose. He'd thought of everything. Had he thought of his answer yet?

The baby continued to make a healthy wail, music to her mother-longing ears. René laid the newborn on Claire's stomach, and pressed to feel for another contraction, then prepared for the afterbirth. Jon held the large stainless-steel basin in readiness.

Jason hovered over Claire and the baby, as they laughed and cried together. René was too busy to hear everything they said, but knew *love* had been mentioned several times. And the name Jason James Rogers, Junior.

She glanced at Jon and saw the familiar look

of wonder that new life always evoked. He met her gaze and held it, adding a smile. Could he read her thoughts, her desires? His short-cropped salt-and-pepper-brown hair had always made his eyes look intense, but she'd never seen that fiery excitement there before. Did he understand how she felt? How every cell in her body cried out for the chance to be a mother?

New life. Nothing compared with the wonder. *Especially if the newborn belongs to you.* Jon glanced back at the happy family, and she prayed they might perform a silent miracle on her behalf.

Jason kissed Claire's forehead, as a distant siren rent the air. René could practically palpate their bonding. There was something about a baby that changed everything, that turned lovers into a family, and sealed a bond outsiders could never fathom. She'd seen it countless times, but this time it plunged straight into her heart.

Her chest clenched and ached for what she longed for, for the answer she depended on to provide the portal to her dreams. She couldn't look at him again for fear she'd beg him to say yes.

"You want to do the honors?" She'd double clamped the umbilical cord and held it with gauze, handing Jason sterile scissors from the suturing pack. For a general practitioner, he looked apprehensive. She gave him an encouraging wink. When he'd finished, she applied the plastic clip on the baby's end of the cord and smiled at the squirming newborn—healthy and strong, though small and a good three weeks premature by her calculations. Babies were nothing short of a miracle; she'd been convinced of that since her first delivery.

There went that clutch in her chest again, the one that made it hard to breathe. She couldn't look at Jon, but felt his gaze on her.

"Congratulations, man," Jon said to Jason. Memories of his wife giving birth flashed before his eyes. Nothing had awed him more, or given him greater satisfaction, than seeing his daughters brought into the world.

He didn't have to look at René to know what she was going through; she'd thoroughly explained her deep hunger for motherhood to him last night. How must it feel to deliver babies for everyone else, and at the end of the day still be alone?

Jason grinned so hard his eyes almost disappeared. Claire patted his hand and welcomed the baby to her chest with the other. From the corner of his eye, Jon watched René's reverent gaze as a pang twisted in his gut. He couldn't take it. Couldn't take the feeling or the implication a simple answer of yes would bring, so he bent to gather the soiled towels and stuff them into the exam room hamper.

The air was too thick with yearning and he'd never been the kind of guy to make dreams come true, just ask his wife. He needed to change the mood. "Do we get paid overtime for this?"

Not usually one to make light, his joke made everyone blurt a relieved laugh. Combined with Claire and Jason's euphoria, joy filled the room from every angle, and against his better judgment, the feel-good rush fueled a growing desire to grant his coworker her biggest wish. He couldn't let it influence him. His decision would be made the same way he made all of his medical determinations, based on logic and common sense. Nothing less.

René looked at him, the makeshift assistant, while the lovebirds and new baby continued bonding. Her expression had changed, as if she understood how much pressure she'd put on him, and how unfairly the perfect timing of this birth had played in her favor. A warm smile appeared on her face, as if the sun had cracked through thunderclouds. How could he not smile back?

"You're not bad for a novice," she said.

So she'd opted to keep it light, too. Relief crawled over him, as if a welcoming blanket. Birth or no birth, he wasn't ready to make his life-altering decision, though her candidness went far to nudge him along.

He flashed a capable look, one that conveyed *I can handle just about anything.* "You're not the only one who's full of surprises, René."

"You want to hold him?" Claire had already dressed her contented-looking baby in blue by early the next morning.

René grinned. "I'd love to." She'd popped in

last night and found Claire sleeping, the baby swaddled and content in the bedside bassinet, and Jason lightly snoring in the lounger, so she tiptoed outside and read the pediatrician's report instead. When the nurses assured her that Claire's fundus was firming right up and there were no signs of excessive bleeding or fever, she'd gone home rather than wake up the new mother and father.

This morning, Jason was already down in the business office settling up, and they'd be heading home to introduce the baby to his big sister, Gina, as soon as René performed her discharge examination.

The six-pound boy squirmed when she took him and tucked him into the hook of her arm. The feel of him sent her reeling. He smelled fresh, like baby lotion and new life, and the clutching in her chest nearly took her breath away. She detected eye movement beneath tightly closed lids with no hint of lashes, and wondered what babies dreamed about. She gently pressed her lips to his head, and inhaled the wonders of his being pure as the first light. The longing in her soul for a baby swelled to near-unbearable proportions. His fine light brown hair resembled a balding man's with a noticeably high forehead. On him it was adorable. Her eyes crinkled as the smile creased her lips.

His tiny hands latched on to her fingers, barely covering the tips. The flood of feelings converged—tingling, prickling, burning—until her eyes brimmed.

Her mouth filled with water, and she swallowed. "He's so beautiful," she whispered, discovering that Claire's eyes shimmered with tears, too.

"I know," Claire said. "Babies are miracles, aren't they?"

Overwhelmed by the moment, wishing for a miracle of her own, her breath got swept away and all René could do was nod.

Jon wolfed down three bagels loaded with peanut butter and downed a pint of orange juice straight out of the carton when he arrived at work. He hadn't slept for a second night, and the usual runner's high had eluded him somewhere around mile eight that morning. He scrubbed his face and strode down the hall.

René was just about to knock on a patient exam room.

"Got a minute?" he said.

She started at his voice and snatched back her hand. "Oh!"

He headed for her office, stopped at the door, tilted his head and arched his eyes to guide her inside.

René's breathing dropped out of sync, coming in gulps. She followed Jon toward her office as tiny invisible wings showered over her head to toe. Oh, God, what would he say?

She stopped one step short of entering the room, swallowed the sock in her throat and gathered her composure. She pasted a smile on her face in hopes of covering her gnawing apprehension, and proceeded inside, then prayed for courage to accept whatever Jon might tell her.

Would she have to go back to plan A, and the donor clinic? God, she hoped not.

"So, I've been thinking," Jon said, the second she stepped over the threshold. "A lot." He engaged her eyes and held her motionless.

"And?" she whispered, closing the door.

"I'm bowled over by this, René. I'd be lying if I didn't say that. I don't understand why you insisted on asking me when Phil is single and available." He held up a hand to stop her before she could begin with the plethora of reasons all over again. She'd recited A to Z quite thoroughly, twice, the night before last. "But I believe your sincerity in wanting this—" he glanced toward the door as if to make sure no one was within hearing range, and though it was closed, he lowered his voice anyway "—baby. I saw it in your eyes last night. This isn't some freaked-out biological-clock whim. This is the real deal."

She nodded her head vehemently.

"I trust you'll stick to your word about my small role in it."

"To the T, Jon. I promise." Oh, heavens, she didn't want to anticipate too much, but it sounded as if he might take her up on the plan. She could only hope and pray. And hold her breath.

"It feels really callous on my part knowing how I plan to take a sabbatical and all, and I care about you as a coworker, and, well, I don't want things to change professionally." He scrubbed his jaw, and the now-familiar facial hair. "This could really ruin our working together."

"I wouldn't want that, either, Jon." Oh, hell, in his swinging pendulum of emotions he'd convinced her from one second to the next to give up on him. Did she really want to sacrifice their professional friendship because of her desire for a baby? Could she blame him for wanting nothing to do with her outrageous plan?

"I'd want to think we could talk things through whenever we needed," he said. "That though I'd be nothing more than a clinical donor as far as the baby goes, I'd like to be your friend. And as a friend and donor I should be able to share in your happiness, like everyone else here in the clinic."

She nodded at his reasonable request, afraid to get too hopeful in case he pulled the rug out from under her dream. "I'd want that, too. I don't want to lose what we have, Jon. Never."

He stepped closer. "What *do* we have, you and me?"

He studied her eyes, making her feel under a microscope. Those winged creatures returned, dropping anxious nectar over the surface of her skin. She took a slow, intentional, quivery breath.

"We have five years of hard work and wonderful achievements to share," she said. "We've laughed, celebrated, mourned and prevailed together over every setback in our clinic." She took a step closer to reach out for his hand. "No matter what happens, if you say yes, you will always be a special friend, Jon." His long fingers laced through hers, still feeling foreign, though warm, regardless of how many times she'd clutched his hand lately.

"No one can know a thing," he cautioned. "If it comes out, I'll leave the clinic."

The importance of anonymity worried her. As with any risk, there was a cost. Was she willing to accept the guilt of changing Jon's future if someone found out? Was she willing to let him pay the price? Confidence leaked out of her pores, leaving her insecure and wobbly. Maybe plan A was the only way to go, but Jon gently stroked her thumb with his, and a silent soothing message transmitted between them.

"I promise," she whispered. A sharp pang in her gut, over the thought of ruining whatever relationship they had, forced her to face the gravity of their possible pact. This was it. Right here, right now. Her dream, their deal, was about to become a reality. The air grew cool and seemed to rush over the surface of her skin, setting off goose bumps.

His molasses-brown gaze swept over her face, as if searching for honesty. Could he look deep enough to see the longings of her heart? She'd meant what she'd said with all of her being.

"After you're pregnant, I want superfriend status." A tiny tug at one corner of his mouth almost turned into a smile.

"You'll do it?" She grabbed his other hand and squeezed both, reeling with hope. The surge pushed her up onto her toes, ready to jump up and down, or kiss his cheek, based on his final decision.

"Yes," he said. "I'll do it."

At the beautiful sound of his reply, she did both.

CHAPTER THREE

THE reward for getting the exquisitely lovely René Munroe to smile was one large dimple and a satisfying hint of an overbite. Jon had once read a study on facial esthetics and found that, in general, men preferred a slight overbite. Come to think of it, seeing her grin like that, he did, too. She'd squealed, jumped up and kissed his cheek when he'd agreed to go through with her plan. She'd kissed him so hard he felt the imprint of her lips half the afternoon. He'd never seen her so animated, and it surprised him, made him wonder how much more there was to know about her.

Since his divorce, after work, he liked his alone time. Preferred it. He'd already done his run for the day and wasn't sure how else to work off this new itchy feeling. And oddly enough, the last thing he felt like being right this minute was alone. Sure he had a day filled with patients ahead of him, but what about after that? He wouldn't get his girls until the weekend.

"You want to go for a coffee after work?" he blurted. The thought of going home to his "man cave"—as his daughters facetiously referred to it—after such a momentous agreement, had little appeal. "We should probably get to know each other a little more."

"That sounds perfect," she said.

Perfect. She used the word frequently, and when it came to describing her it suited...well...it suited her perfectly.

"I'll see you later, then," he said, heading for the door with a new spring in his jogging shoes.

At the end of the workday, they locked the clinic and hiked the two blocks over to State Street, and caught the electric trolley heading north to an alfresco coffeehouse. They'd committed to coffee, not dinner. It was a start. Even though it was late January, the temperature was sixty-five degrees, and the outdoor restaurants all had outdoor heating lamps for their patrons' comfort. If he inhaled deep enough, he could smell the crisp, tangy sea.

"Do you ever get tired of delivering babies?" he asked, as they rode.

"No. It's wonderful, isn't it?"

Jon nodded and thought back to the birth of both of his daughters. Amanda had been born at a midwife center eighteen years back, and Lacy, at home, under water, eighteen months later. His ex-wife had wanted it that way. He'd felt as if he'd run a marathon after each labor and delivery, but had never been more ecstatic in his life. Watching Jason and Claire last night had brought back long-forgotten memories.

Somehow lecturing patients about their tickers didn't quite measure up, though of course he understood the importance of the heart sustaining life. It just couldn't quite compare with the theatrical bang of a delivery.

"I never thought I'd see Jason happy again," she said.

Hmm? Oh, he'd taken a tangential thought trip, and quickly focused back in. "I guess there's hope for all of us, then," Jon said, deciding, on a scale of one to ten, he probably sat around six on the happy meter—not ecstatic, not miserable, just making due, especially since his divorce.

He'd forgotten what this type of elation felt like, being more used to the endorphin variety from his long and hard runner workouts. Emotional highs were…well…unusual these days. Definitely nice, but different.

He glanced at René smiling with cheeks blushed from her hard work and the brisk evening air. Her amber eyes hinted at green, probably because of the teal-colored sweater she wore. *As a pool reflects the sky, light eyes reflect surrounding colors.* Where had he recently read that, and why had he lost his train of thought again?

"You've sure made me a happy camper," she said, with a perky glance out the window, which made her earrings sway.

Never having been in the business of granting wishes before, he enjoyed the swell of pride and rode along with it.

He noticed René always wore extralong earrings, and right now the colorful beads and loops almost reached her shoulders, and for some odd reason it fascinated him the way they swayed with the movement of her head. Mesmerizing. But that was neither here nor there; he was on a mission to get to know René better, not notice her earrings or how they swayed with her long, thick hair. There had to be some relevant question he could think of to ask.

For the life of him, he couldn't figure out why a woman such as René wasn't happily married. She should be having a baby with her doting husband instead of soliciting his services.

His services? The thought tickled the corner of his mouth into a near smile and he looked straight ahead so she wouldn't notice. He'd really agreed to do this crazy thing. For René. Two years ago, when Cherie had kicked him to the curve without so much as a hint of being discontent, who would have ever thought about agreeing to such a ridiculous idea? That smile kept edging up his face, and he kept staring out the front window to hide it.

When they reached their stop, they hopped off the trolley, walked half a block and ordered their brews at the shop, then sat outside to enjoy the clear evening sky. In the distance, he could see the lights flicker on Stearns Wharf and wished he could hear the waves crashing against the pilings.

Beneath her shrouded gaze, René sat quietly, as if waiting for him to break the ice, to bring up the next step in their plan—admittedly, the trickiest, as far as he was concerned.

Not ready to go there yet, Jon took a drink of espresso and winced at the bitterness. "Since we don't know much about each other, I'll start. My girls are both in high school. Amanda's going to graduate this June, and Lacy next year. Amanda has applied to every Ivy League school she could think of since she's got it in her head that, if she wants to go to Harvard Law, she's got to do her undergraduate studies at an equally prestigious school."

Everyone in the medical clinic was well aware of his divorce two years earlier, how hard it had hit. But no one could possibly know, since he'd worked extrahard at hiding it, how devastated he'd been. How he never saw himself ever loving again, beyond his daughters. They'd seen the happy family guy turn into his current recluse status, and he'd complained bitterly to anyone who would listen about how Cherie had practically cleaned him out financially. But he'd always stopped short of the point of how he didn't think he could go on, and how he never ever wanted to commit to another relationship because of it.

On a more practical note, he didn't need to bore René with the difficulty of supporting his family at the level to which they'd become accustomed, while living on his own and saving for both daughters' college funds.

Still, having taken the business risk with his colleagues and opened the clinic, he'd refused to bail for a higher-paying job when Cherie demanded the outrageous monthly alimony. The clinic was all about autonomy, which mattered a lot to him. It was all he had left. That same autonomy was what fueled his sabbatical dreams.

René sipped her tea concoction as coils of steam circled her face. He could smell the peppermint all the way across the table. She lifted intriguingly shaped brows, brows he'd never really noticed before now.

"And Lacy?" she asked. "What are her plans?"

Jon barked a laugh. "She's thinking more in line with Oahu U." He made the "hang loose" hand gesture associated with the laidback Hawaiian Islands. "My girls couldn't be more different if they tried." He shook his head, knowing both daughters had genius IQs. Sometimes he wondered if his genes were a blessing or a curse.

"As long as they're happy, right?" she said.

He nodded wholeheartedly. Ah, to be young and free to start over again, but happiness was such a subjective state of being. At forty-two he was the picture of health, which should make him happy, yet sometimes he felt unnecessarily weighted down by responsibility. At times like that, his sabbatical plans helped keep him going.

Since divorcing and moving out, he'd occupied eight hundred square feet of high-tech loft where he practiced urban minimalism. His daughters were the ones to name it the "man cave." As long as he had his books and stereo equipment, and visitation rights with his girls, he'd make do—even if he couldn't satisfactorily explain the temporary feel of his current living situation.

She watched him closely, forcing him to say something. Anything. "And I suppose this deal we're making will make you happy?" he said.

With warm eyes hinting at wisdom well beyond her thirty-plus years, René studied him as if on the verge of telling her deepest secret. That near-perfect smile stretched across her face. "You have no idea."

The moments yawned on with the two of them cautiously watching each other. She told him how her parents had retired and moved to Nevada. How she was an only child. How all of her best friends were married and how she always felt like the odd woman out whenever they got together. He asked where the men in her life had all gone. Her relaxed expression became peppered with annoyance.

He knew the war chant—men, the callous heart-breakers! He could repeat the same, only changing the gender. Yet he wanted her to open up, to tell him something personal, so he bit his tongue. If they were going to make a baby together, he felt he had the right to know more about her.

"Ten years ago, I'd thought I'd found my soul

mate, but instead, he dumped me, crushing my heart beneath his feet as he walked out the door." She glanced at him. Could she tell he knew exactly how she felt? "Sorry for sounding overdramatic, but that's how it felt. Since then, I've had a series of less-than-satisfying relationships, and I'm pessimistic when it comes to the topic of permanent love."

Jon had been married so long, and hadn't pursued much in the way of romantic relationships since his divorce out of commitment fears, but he'd heard enough women around the clinic moan about the same thing. Love and permanence didn't seem to fit. He figured the world of dating wasn't such a great place to be these days, but for the life of him and his old-school ways, he couldn't figure out what kind of guy would let a woman like René get away.

Watching René sip her tea, Jon figured the ticking of her biological clock influenced her every thought. Sure, lots of women were waiting until their early forties to have their first babies, but she'd have to risk the time to find the right guy, get married and get pregnant when it was a well-known fact that fertility declined with each year after thirty. She'd made it very clear she wasn't willing to take the chance. He'd computed that if she waited much longer, she'd be in her late fifties with teenagers, and that thought, having two teenagers himself, gave him pause. It was all luck anyway, and if he knew one thing about René, it was that she wasn't a gambler. If she was going to respond to her brewing and strengthening desire for motherhood, she'd have to act…well, soon.

"Have you really given up on finding the right guy?" He lifted his brows, prodding, then when she didn't immediately answer, he switched to a more challenging look.

Her gaze danced away. "Not completely."

Since she wasn't about to open up, he let slip a sudden thought. "Someone like you could make the right guy very happy, but after you have a baby—" *my baby;* the quick thought took him by surprise and not unpleasantly "—it may be more difficult to find him."

"Who?" she asked.

"Him. The right guy."

"Having a baby on my own may not seem like the perfect solution, but it's what I want. I don't need a man to validate me. And if the consequences are being a single mother, I'll deal with them like a big girl."

For the third time in as many days she placed her hand on top of his. Her warmth enveloped his and on reflex he responded and twined his fingers through hers. This handholding business was starting to feel normal. His eyes latched on to her almost-caramel gaze and held it, unwavering.

She squeezed his hand. "You're giving me the most important gift I've ever wanted. How will I ever be able to thank you?"

He thought long and hard about the right response. He thought about the greatest gift in his life—his daughters—and though his answer might come off as being lame, he meant it. "You can thank me by being a good mother."

René had pulled the lucky straw when it came to choosing offices. Hers was in the front of the American version of the Queen Anne Victorian house. The three-story, cream-colored structure proudly bore the official Santa Barbara historical site emblem. Her corner office was nestled in the polygonal-shaped tower, which came complete with ceiling-to-floor bay windows. She'd covered them in sheer white lace, and loved how the sun danced in patterns across the walls in the afternoons.

She'd splurged on a Chinese-inspired walnut desk with cabriole legs, and one huge Oriental rug over the wood floor. The office seemed more befitting of a princess than a middle-class girl from Tustin, California.

Her parents had cashed in early on her brains, and scholarships flowed throughout her high school and college years. She'd never relied on anything but hard work and innovative thinking to get her through, though many attributed her success to her looks rather than sweat and elbow grease. It didn't seem worth the effort to hold a grudge for their uncharitable assumptions.

She'd tried her best to be the perfect daughter, the perfect student, the perfect girlfriend—that one had never paid off—and the perfect medical practice partner and doctor. The last required long hours and dedication to the clinic, and left little room for a normal social life. Now, thanks to Jon's decision, she could skip over all of the preliminaries and have her shot at motherhood.

His one request? To be a good mother. He hadn't said perfect mother, no, just a *good* one. A good-enough mother. And that's what she'd try with all of her heart to be.

A rap at her door, followed by her nurse escorting her next patient into the office for a consultation, forced her out of the all-consuming thoughts.

After greetings, René engaged the tension-filled eyes of her last patient of the day. The woman sat across from her desk wringing her hands. Her husband sat waiting beside her, straight as a giraffe, eyes more like a hawk.

"I'll get right to it," René said and smiled, fingering a printout report. "I received your endometrial biopsy results this morning, and they were benign." She smiled again, and noticed that relief hadn't washed away the couple's furrowed brows and apprehensive eyes. "That means it was negative. You're clean. No more cancer."

The middle-aged patient and her husband shared a sigh, smiled and hugged. The scene made René wish all her medical "news" could be as good.

After they stood and shook hands, and René had instructed the patient to stop by Gaby's desk and make a follow-up appointment, she folded her arms and paced the room. She was at her prime, in excellent physical condition, and good health should never be taken for granted. Now was the perfect time…for…

Her eyes drifted to the one wall reserved for every baby she'd ever delivered. The ever-growing collage of pictures—big and small, ornate and plain—called out to her. She scanned the gallery and thought again about becoming a mother. Chills tickled her neck.

She sat at her desk, stared at the detailed crown molding along the ceiling and tapped a light rhythm with her pen. More exciting thoughts about parenthood whispered through her mind. Her dream really could come true. She could barely wait.

With her restless gaze wandering the expanse of the office, she nibbled a fingernail, while her crossed leg pumped a breakneck beat. On the opposite wall was a framed photograph of the four MidCoast Medical partners the day the clinic had opened. She meandered over and took the picture in her hands. They all smiled. She was flanked by Jon on one side and Philip on the other, and next to Jon stood Jason, the owner of the building. The day was one of the happiest of her life. She remembered hugging each of them, and sharing a bottle of champagne. She thought about the hope they all had, and the desire to serve the local Santa Barbara community, back before Jason's wife and daughter had died and Jon was still happily married.

She'd expected to marry, too, but life had surprised them all. Only Philip, the happy bachelor, seemed to make it through the past five years unscathed.

Well, it was her chance now. The sperm bank had called to tell her Jon had made an appointment for today—Valentine's Day! He had skipped part of his morning clinic for an appointment, and she'd quietly chuckled over the reason—to donate his sperm, designated for her. But when it hit her between the eyes that her dream was about to come true, the gesture touched her so deeply she'd flat-out cried. Now she grinned and shook her head. Jon was right about two things: he was full of surprises, and no matter what happened after this, their relationship would never be the same.

Who knows how long she stared at the photograph. Jon's image made her smile. His lanky frame, angular features, friendly demeanor and over-the-top intelligence gave her confidence she'd chosen the right man, and right now, she owed him another gigantic thank-you. And maybe another home-cooked meal?

Jon stared down Antonin Grosso. The stocky man sat across from his desk with arms folded, and a stubborn glint in his eyes.

"Your thallium treadmill showed an abnormality suggestive of arterial blockage."

The man scrubbed his face with a beefy

hand. "Please, doctor, I'm a butcher—speak the English!"

Jon grimaced. True, layman's terms were his downfall. "You may have a blocked artery in your heart. I can't stress enough the need for an angiogram. Oh, uh, that's a study that will tell me if any of your heart arteries *are* blocked." He fished through his patient education pamphlets and found the right one, then handed it to him.

"I no need this test. I feel fine."

"Feeling fine and being fine are two different things, Mr. Grosso." Jon ran his hand over his stiff spiky hair and reconsidered the explanation in butcher's vernacular. "Take your prime beef. It may look fine, but until the U.S. government checks it out and approves it, you won't know if it's diseased or not." He stared at the man while the analogy computed. "You look good. You feel good. But your heart isn't so good. This study says so. We may need to unplug the arteries so your heart gets more blood and feels better."

Something clicked. The man's expression brightened. "You mean like that plumbing guy? My pipes need cleaning?"

Jon snapped his fingers and pointed at Mr. Grosso. "Exactly! Your pipes may need cleaning out. We need to schedule an appointment for a special test to decide if they do."

"I don't know. That sounds dangerous. I need to talk to my wife first."

"Okay. Talk to your wife, but make it soon. I'll talk to her, too, if you'd like. Bottom line—you need this test, Mr. Grosso."

"Okay, okay, but I feel fine." He rose to leave, and Jon stood, too.

"It's Friday. I want to hear from you by next Wednesday." Jon waved the EKG and treadmill results around to impress the patient that he had solid proof he needed the angiogram. "You have to get this done ASAP."

The man glanced over his shoulder, then hung his head when he grabbed the doorknob. "We'll see," he mumbled.

Jon sat on the edge of his solid oak behemoth of a desk and shook his head. Before he had the chance to mutter a single curse, something grabbed his attention, and two young ladies rushed him.

"Dad!"

"Hi, Daddy!"

Amanda and Lacy threw their arms around him and hung tight. Every frustrated physician-oriented thought he'd been thinking flew out of his head. His teenage daughters had a way of doing that for him.

"Hey!" he said, smiling. "You guys are early."

"Mom had a hot date," Lacy said, with a strong hint of sarcasm.

Ack. Cherie hadn't even tried to hide her multiple trysts from the girls since the divorce. Hell, she'd started extramarital dating before they'd even finalized the divorce. The thought still boiled his blood.

While deep in a group hug, he noticed René walk up to his door. Her intent expression changed to comprehension when she spied the girls. Since his office was in the back of the building, and the copying machines and bathrooms were in the middle, he knew she only came to this part of the clinic if she needed to talk to him.

She shook her head and flipped her hand in a wave, mouthed "thank you" and started to walk away. The sparkle in her eyes, since he'd agreed to be her sperm donor, had made everyone in the clinic take note. He'd heard his nurses comment to each other. "What's up with Dr. Munroe?" "I wonder if she's in love!"

His daughters turned their heads toward the door and caught sight of René just as she turned to leave. "I just wanted to wish you a happy Valentine's Day, Jon," she said, expertly covering for herself.

"Hey, same to you."

He grinned at the thought of having put that gleam in her flashing eyes. Briefly, he wondered what would have transpired if his daughters hadn't arrived early. Would she give him another squeeze of the hand and kiss on the cheek, a gorgeously grateful smile, and eyes so filled with joy his heart would palpitate? He felt guilty how simple his part of the agreement was, but if she wanted to make this huge deal out of it, it was fine with him. As long as no one found out. As long as it wouldn't change his life or routine, or plans for China.

"Who was that?" Lacy asked.

"You know, Dr. Munroe. She's one of the partners," he said. He continued the group hug with the girls, and smiled.

"She's really pretty," Amanda said.

"Why don't you ask her out?" Lacy added.

"A date?" He made an incredulous laugh. "Who needs that when I've already got my favorite girls?"

Even if it would cost him a dinner out and involve some sort of shoes or clothes shopping, he wouldn't trade his biweekly visitation weekends with his daughters for anything in the world. Especially on the most interesting Valentine's Day he'd had in a long time.

CHAPTER FOUR

MONDAY morning, René had to teach the last "What to Expect When Expecting" class since Claire had delivered prematurely. Ten women in various stages of pregnancy sat rapt with attention at the day's topic: Epidural or Natural Birth. René already knew what her personal preference would be. Natural birth.

One woman was unfamiliar to René, and since only MidCoast Medical patients, in particular her OB/Gyn patients could participate, she questioned her.

"Oh, I'm Gretchen, Stephanie Ingram's doula. She was called into court today."

The lawyer was involved in a high-profile murder case, and René had often lamented about the horrible timing of it with her pregnancy.

Hmm, a doula. Stephanie had hired an assistant to provide nonmedical support during the pregnancy and delivery. Claire had recommended her. The doula would perform nonmedical duties—anything from back rubs to aromatherapy, to errands, or anything else the future mom might need. The doula's goal was to organize and support the mother through the entire process. *Sounds like something I may require in the near future, if all goes well.* It was never too soon to plan ahead.

"May I have your business card?" René asked.

Gretchen Lingstrom—freckled, redheaded, tattooed and eyebrow pierced—beamed as she handed her the card.

After the class had ended, René searched out Jon. She wanted to bring him up to date on the chat with her lawyer. Both of his exam rooms were closed, which meant he was seeing a patient.

She peeked around the corner of his door. He sat, head down, scribbling away with his left hand. For an out-of-this-stratosphere smart guy, he definitely had an artistic side. One thing she remembered was that he kept a journal, and it was something she'd always admired about him. He'd admitted it to her at the first clinic

Christmas party after his divorce, where he'd had a bit too much to drink. He'd clearly been hurting at the time, and said it helped him relieve stress and work through his divorce. She'd never realized how hard his divorce had been on him until the other night, when they'd set out to get to know each other after agreeing to make a baby together. She wondered if he was writing about how backward their process was.

René smiled and tapped on the door. Her stomach went quivery and her heart bumped up its rhythm, and she didn't understand why.

"Hey," he said, a welcoming gleam in his eyes.

"Hey. I just wanted to bring you up-to-date. I got word the…uh…specimen made the grade. We're all set to go as soon as I—" she glanced down the hall and back, then whispered "—ovulate."

Surprisingly, his cheeks rouged up as he gave her a lightbulb broad smile and a thumbs-up sign.

That afternoon, Mrs. Grosso stood somber faced before Jon, with Antonin doing his best to hide behind her four-foot-eleven frame. "He no want the test. It's too much. Too dangerous."

"Mrs. Grosso, are you aware that your husband could die from a heart attack if he doesn't take care of his arteries?"

She glanced over her shoulder; Antonin made such a minute head shake only his eyes seemed to move. She let go a long string of emphatic Italian words, obviously berating him for denying that fact prior to now.

"No. No. No," Antonin said. He couldn't be swayed.

Worry etched her brow as she shrugged. "What I'm going to do?"

Jon looked into his patient's eyes. "If I make an appointment for an ultrasound of the heart, where they just bounce sound waves off your chest, will you go?"

"No cutting? No needles?" the man said.

Jon shook his head. "If you see for yourself there is a blockage, will you promise to have the test—the real test—to save your life?"

The missus poured out more Italian, this time using her hands and arms for accentuation.

Antonin's grumpy face took on a more thought-ful expression.

"You'll already be in the hospital and we can handle things from there. What do you say?" Jon said.

The man stared at the floor and mumbled, "Oh-kay."

Jon clapped his hands. "That's the spirit." He hopped behind his desk and punched in a phone number. "Let's see how soon I can arrange the ultrasound." *For the walking time bomb.*

He got put on hold, used his index finger to play with the silly little patch of hair under his lower lip. The patch his girls had insisted he grow. They said it would make him look sexy. He almost laughed out loud. Did a man want to look sexy at forty-two? A really odd thought occurred to him. If René had handpicked him to be her donor, was there anything about him she found sexy besides his DNA?

He squashed the thought immediately. The last thing he wanted was to foul up his plans for free-dom with any kind of commitment.

As he waited on hold, and the Grossos spoke

in excitable Italian, hands and gestures flying, his mind drifted to the vision of René at his door that morning. She wore a little white sweater over her earth-tone patterned sheath dress. The half-sleeved sweater with a shiny bead-and-stud design up the front had been the perfect accessory. He'd noticed that about her. She was good with details.

And he liked that. Liked that he knew she'd always do a job thoroughly, down to the miniscule touches. He thought about the dinner she'd made the night she'd asked him to be her sperm donor—she cooked that way, too. Whenever they had potlucks at work from now on, he'd twist her arm to cook. There was something in the way she combined herbs and spices that made her dishes exceptional. If she weren't such a fantastic doctor, he might suggest she'd missed her calling, but if she'd become a chef, he'd never have met her.

An uncomfortable feeling spun in his stomach. These were useless thoughts, fanciful thoughts, that a man with plans for a sabbatical shouldn't bother to have. As he continued to wait to speak to a hospital operator, he thumbed through his journal, past the part detailing life's recent surprising turn, and back to his list of cities in China that he planned to visit after he attended the world cardiac conference in Beijing—2011; the year of the rabbit.

In light of the new circumstances, for some dumb reason, the year of the rabbit struck him funny.

The following Saturday morning, René rode her bicycle on a different route, along the Cabrillo Boulevard bike path. The early morning air was crisp and the sun bright. She squinted, despite wearing sunglasses. Up ahead on the palm-tree-lined path, a tall, fit figure ran at a near sprinter's pace. From the crowd of joggers, she'd recognize him anywhere.

She'd never seen Jon jogging, and definitely had never seen him shirtless before. It shook her a little. His musculature surprised her, too. Intrigued her. Long waisted, like a swimmer, his shoulders were broad and his upper arms were surprisingly buff. Jon? His stomach was flat and obviously no stranger to crunches. Another surprise. Long solid legs finished off his six-foot frame, and carried him at a rapid clip along the shore.

He concentrated on his run, and didn't see or recognize her when she pedaled toward him. Maybe it was the bike helmet? Vanity prompted her to take it off and fluff out her hair before she called his name.

"Jon!" She waved.

His pace stuttered, he turned and followed the sound.

"Jon! Hi!"

He waved and ran off the path, circling back toward her. "What's up?"

"Just enjoying the sunny morning."

"Yeah, it's beautiful today, isn't it."

As they chitchatted, she worked hard at concentrating on his face so he wouldn't think she was checking him out. His gaze passed over her shorts-clad legs once or twice. What was that about?

A large group of cyclists advanced, so she cut things short.

"I just wanted to thank you again for…you know."

"Ah," he said, suddenly finding his running shoes fascinating. "That."

They exchanged a secret-handshake kind of look, something that was quickly becoming routine.

"Yeah. That. You know how grateful I am."

"Yep."

"Okay. Well, I'll see you Monday," she said.

He nodded and waved. She noticed the well-formed muscle ripple up his arm and shoulder, and couldn't stop herself from waiting until he'd run off before putting her cycle helmet back on. Once she'd set off, she couldn't resist a glance over her shoulder for the back view. She swerved and had to put her foot down to keep from falling. But it was worth it! A straight spine with triangular muscles fanning across his back, flexed with the natural swing of his arms. His torso angled down to trim hips and a backside barely covered by his shorts. Never in a million years would she have imagined him to look this hot. She'd come to a dead stop and soon realized several more cyclists were headed her way, so she pushed off and continued in the opposite direction.

She'd been up all night thinking about Jon. Not in a sexual way. No. But in a new and different light—a beam of potential. Seeing him like this mixed her up, especially now, when things were moving ahead as planned.

She had nothing but respect for Jon Becker. They'd been through a lot together launching the medical practice. She remembered how flattered she'd been when Jason and Jon had approached her about joining them on the venture. She'd only been board certified in OB/Gyn for a year and yet they'd invited her to take a chance on a new direction for her career, one where she had more say and control. She remembered blinking two or three times and saying yes! And she hadn't looked back or regretted it since.

She'd almost broached the subject foremost on her mind with Jon last Friday afternoon, just to tell him thanks for what seemed like the hundredth time in the past few weeks, but he'd been waylaid by his girls. She'd caught them in a cuddle with the oldest, Amanda, sporting a sleek dark-brown bob, kissing his cheek, and the honey-haired Lacy, with wild shoulder-length curls, snuggling his chest. He never looked happier than when he was with them. A prerequisite for what they'd planned was that it couldn't affect his relationship with his girls in any way. They'd never know, and she'd do anything to keep it that way.

René pedaled beyond the beach volleyball courts toward the pond. Her mind wandered back to Jon as the hodgepodge of her thoughts practically made her eyes cross. They'd worked closely together for five years. Not only was he a person she admired and trusted, he was a genius, and ethically minded—a great combination for father material. She had nothing but respect for him and cared about him as a friend. To admit he was a damn fine specimen of a man on top of everything else was far too confusing.

No way would she allow herself to examine that freshly discovered secret. Even though he'd looked fantastic in those jogging shorts, there was no place for emotion in this plan.

She circled the pond and headed toward home. She'd been tracking her menstrual cycle for the past few months, and if all went well, she'd be ovulating next week. Deep in thought, she glanced up and nearly screamed. A four-seat bicycle surrey almost ran her off the road. She veered from the path and onto the grass, and stopped just before rolling over the curb and into the street, heavy with fast-moving traffic. Once she regained her breath she got right back on the bike and pedaled faster.

If she got herself killed, she wouldn't be able to get inseminated!

The following week, Jon's morning cardiac clinic had been brutal. One complication after another—a surprise diagnosis or three, word of a cardiac arrest of one of his oldest patients and then he'd had to break the news to Katerina and Antonin Grosso that, after having the echocardiogram, Antonin definitely needed a triple bypass graft, *molto presto*.

Just before noon, as Jon discussed the pros and cons of blood pressure medicine with his newest cardiac patient, his intercom buzzed.

It was René. "I've got the contract. Can you meet me at Stearns Wharf for lunch today?"

"Sure," he said, pleased about the prospect of seeing her away from work again.

She gave him the time and hung up.

He'd managed to compartmentalize the whole artificial insemination agreement since the day she'd dropped the überbaby bomb. But the call shook him out of his complacency, his heart *lub-dubbed* more per minute than usual and he held the receiver with a suddenly moist palm. There was no way he could convince himself his part in their deal was insignificant when a new life might be created as a result.

He scratched his forehead, and remembered he had a patient sitting across from him. "Yes. Well, let's discuss beta blockers versus calcium channel blockers."

The patient's expression drew a blank. "Sorry," Jon said, then stated a brand name for each drug classification he'd mentioned and noticed an ember of understanding in his patient's previous dull gaze. Together, they chose the best medicine suited for his condition and lifestyle, and when at the end of the appointment they shook hands, the patient thanked Jon profusely.

The morning seemed to drag on, while Jon had second, third and even fourth thoughts about actually going through with the contract. He remembered the bright spark of hope in René's eyes when he'd agreed, and relived the unbridled excitement when she'd hurled herself into his arms, hugged the wind out of him, then kissed his cheek so hard he swore he felt her lips there the rest of the day.

He smiled. He could make René's dream come true. How often in life did a man get that kind of opportunity with no strings attached? He thought about his daughters and how much he loved them. How parental love surpassed romantic love, at least it had in his marriage. While marital love might weaken and fade away, the love of a child grew stronger every day. The joy those girls had brought to his life went beyond measure, and René deserved her chance to experience the same.

He removed his doctor's coat, replacing it with a lightweight bomber-style jacket for the crisp February day, and set off on foot to meet René at the wharf after her morning surgi-clinic at the local outpatient center.

As he approached their agreed-upon restaurant, the crunching and creaking of the wooden planks from behind made him turn. He spotted her car. She'd been lucky enough to find a parking place on the often-overcrowded wharf. A nervous zing buzzed through his system, and he quickly ignored it. He was a man of his word—he'd made a promise; he couldn't back out now. After all, he'd already given the specimen!

The cornflower-blue sky went on forever, an occasional cloud scudding past. The sun glare ricocheted off the ocean, making it hard to see anything beyond her silhouette as she got out of the car. She walked closer, and the beam on her face matched the shimmering waves. The sun kissed her chestnut hair, highlighting a touch of red he hadn't noticed before. She tucked her arm through the crook of his elbow like an ambassador of goodwill.

"Lunch is on me," she said, as the wharf's resident pelican swooped overhead and landed on the nearby railing.

Over a bucket of all-you-can-peel shrimp, she produced a manila envelope and withdrew its contents. "I've pored over this document, every single line, and I think you'll be pleased with what my lawyer drew up."

He wiped his hands on a napkin and maintained her steady gaze and ceremoniously accepted the contract, then fished his reading glasses out from his shirt pocket.

"Once I've got your signature, they'll release your specimen to me."

By the time the main course of halibut and mahimahi got served, he'd signed it.

"That's that, then," he said, glancing up, noticing the glassy tears threatening to spill over her thick lashes. Oh, no. He could never take it when a woman cried. It always made him feel so helpless and baffled and downright uncomfortable. His girls had mastered the art of tearful manipulation, but René's tears were genuine. He'd do anything to stop them, but what?

Though he thought better of it, he did what he'd do with Amanda, scooted closer and gave René a hug. She clutched him so hard, he wasn't sure whether to pry himself free or just enjoy it.

"Thank you," she repeated over and over.

"I've got to admit I'm very curious how this puppy's gonna turn out."

"Me, too!" More tears appeared—tasteful tears, not the blubbering kind, just gracious, womanly drops down her cheeks. On her, it was beautiful and he had the urge to kiss each one away, but that would be him in a movie, not the real guy sitting here next to her, the guy who worked with her every day, so he stopped the urge immediately. Still wanting nothing more than to stop her crying, he took the joker route.

He covered his mouth with the back of his hand, and mumbled an aside. "Okay, I've done my part. Now it's your turn."

She sputtered a laugh and tossed him a thankful look, one that seemed to wrap him up and warm him all over again. The gaze let him know he was the most special person in her life at the moment. He liked how it felt, wondered if she sensed the ever-deepening place she'd found in his life, too. It confused the hell out of him. The moment couldn't go on forever, and they did have a delicious-smelling lunch before them, and, well, he scooted his chair back as the special feeling settled quietly in his chest.

A week later, after the most recent blood test showed a surge in René's luteinizing hormone, indicative of ovulation, she canceled her morning appointments and rushed to her OB doctor's office. She lay on a cold examination table with her feet in stirrups.

She glanced at the ceiling with a new perspective on the patient's side of the experience. The room was cold and the thin sheet offered little comfort on top of the oversize patient gown. Her personal gynecologist smiled at her from between René's legs.

"Ready?" she said.

René nodded, her throat growing tight with anticipation.

She and Jon had agreed not to discuss the mechanics of their situation. He'd done his part when the time suited him, and now she'd do hers. She still laughed to herself about how he'd made his deposit on Valentine's Day. Could she consider it romantic?

"Here it is," her doctor said, raising a thin catheter connected to a syringe with the sperm inside. "Future baby, right here, if we're lucky."

The doctor chattered as René felt cold hands and necessary invasive instruments get placed, and finally the deposited sperm around her cervix.

"I'm going to put a sponge cap over your cervix. Leave it in place for eight hours." Her doctor friend patted her hip. "Good luck. Now lay here for thirty minutes. My nurse will let you know when you can get up."

If there was a chant to will one sperm and her egg to meet, she'd chant it. Failure was not an option. She pulled her feet out of the stirrups, moved farther up the exam table and relaxed.

Maybe daydreaming about a perfect ending would enhance the process. In her case the perfect ending was a pregnancy.

She let her mind wander and, instead of a chubby baby face appearing, a different scene played out before her, shocking her slightly. She'd told Jon that Mr. Right wasn't going to walk through her door anytime soon, yet the vision of him standing on her porch the night she'd hit him up with her artificial insemination plans gave her pause. In a once removed and cockeyed sort of way, he *was* Mr. Right.

She couldn't help but wonder if in another situation, if she wasn't pushing so hard for a baby *right now* and if he wasn't counting down the days to his freedom, that maybe things could have been different between them. In all their years of working together, they'd never once looked at each other in an interested way. And it was useless to speculate about things that would never be. She didn't have the luxury of time anyway, and this day was what it was—a day to hold her breath, keep a positive attitude and hope for the best.

And if optimism could affect her state of mind and the cells in her body and, most importantly, her uterus, she figured she had the best chance ever to get pregnant.

CHAPTER FIVE

JON hadn't been intentionally avoiding René for the past month, but he'd figured he'd done his part in their deal, and there was no point in making her uncomfortable just because he was curious. Beyond curious. Besides, he didn't want to get involved.

Since he'd donated and signed her contract, he'd stayed out of her way and figured things would play themselves out however they were meant to be. It surprised him to acknowledge—as a scientist first and foremost—he could be so fatalistic. Since agreeing to take part in René's plan, he'd started realizing all kinds of new things about himself. Such as, he really, really hoped this pregnancy would take.

What was up with that?

Jon welcomed his next patient into the exam

room as if a special guest. "Mr. Grosso, how are you doing?"

"Not so great." The man gingerly rubbed his chest.

Mrs. Grosso beetled her brows. "He still tender."

"Yeah, tender." He massaged circles around his sternum.

"That was a big operation, and right about now your skin nerve endings are coming back to life in the area where they opened your chest."

"It feels strange. I can't explain."

"But you're not having chest pain, right?"

"No. No chest pain. Just sore now."

"That's progress. Take off your shirt and let's have a look."

After performing a thorough examination, Jon invited Antonin to get dressed and meet him in his office. He exited the room and strode toward his door. On the way, he noticed René with a bright smile, standing at the mouth of the hall. He slowed his step. She gave him a subtle thumbs-up.

What? He did a double take to make sure he

hadn't imagined it. He tilted his head as if for reassurance that she had indeed given the high sign. She nodded rapidly, continuing to smile so wide she could star in a commercial for toothpaste.

He went to his office and picked up the phone, punching in her com line number. After the second ring she picked up.

"Are you saying you're pregnant?" *It took on the first try?*

"Yes!" Her excitement burst through the receiver.

A moment lapsed, as a swell of something bathed him. Joy? Pride? Nah, that would be absurd, but, hey, *it took on the first try!* "I think this calls for celebration," he said.

"Definitely." She sounded breathless.

"I've got a bottle of nonalcoholic sparkling cider the girls didn't drink on New Year's. How about tonight at eight. My house."

"See you there." She hung up.

"Congratulations," Mrs. Grosso said, while assisting her husband into his office.

"For what?"

"You wife. She pregnant?"

"Oh. No. Just a friend of mine."

Mrs. Grosso still knew how to look coy. "Your girlfriend?"

"Just a friend."

He shuffled the stack of lab reports on his desk and waited for the couple to settle in. It might prove harder than he originally thought to keep a secret about the fact that he had something to do with René's pregnancy.

René tapped on Jon's steel door five minutes early. It sounded like a vault opening, and he must have been waiting just on the other side, it opened so quickly.

"Hey," he said, eyes bright. His black tailored shirt, with sleeves rolled to his forearms, hugged his trim, long torso. The jeans fit just right, too. She'd noticed he'd shaved off his beard earlier in the week and missed it, but evening stubble darkened his face. The image set off a burst of excitement on an already-overloaded day. She chalked it up to fatigue mixed with euphoria.

"Hey," she replied as she entered his loft. The perfectly square main room was decorated with

clean urban minimalism, and surprisingly unusual artwork balanced out the sparse furniture.
Dare she say sensual artwork, with warm and inviting shapes and colors? She scanned the room,
and noticed an alcove separated by a Japanese
paper screen that was most likely his bedroom. A
closed door next to it she pegged as the bathroom.
The mantel sans fireplace came complete with a
large mirror and—she had to look twice—larger
than life-size angel-wing artifacts? Jon?

"My daughters tease me about that one, too," he
said as a smile slid across his face. "Found them
in Venice. Couldn't resist. The shipping fee was
astounding."

A laugh tickled up from deep inside. She imagined Jon in Italy making plans to ship his art
home, using sign language and pointing to the
wings. Then another peculiar thought popped into
her mind about him and Cherie dividing up their
property during the divorce, and Jon insisting he
keep those serene angel wings. What kind of man
would want to look at angel wings every day? She
smiled at him, a man who'd already proved himself as an angel. It felt good to be here, to share

the news she'd been bursting to tell the world all day.

She followed him toward the spotless new kitchen wedged into the far corner of the completely undivided room. Her eyes bugged out at the conference-size black-enameled dining table, and how he'd taken over half of it with his computer equipment.

"Do you entertain a lot?" This was certainly a side she'd never seen of Jon.

"Me? Are you kidding? Nah, I just like how it fits here, and the girls really spread out with their books and laptops and all. It works for us."

"It's impressive how much thought you put into the girls when you moved here."

"As you'll soon find out, kids become the biggest part of your life. Even bigger than medicine. It's great."

He retrieved the alcohol-free sparkling cider from the ice bucket and popped the cork faster than she could blink. "Let's toast to our success."

"Yes, of course! That's what I came here to do, to celebrate."

That devilish sparkle she sometimes noticed

appeared in his eyes. "I have to know one thing," he said. "Was it as good for you as it was for me?"

She sputtered a laugh and delivered a firm sock to his deltoid. Feeling a bit like a schoolgirl again, she rolled her eyes at his tasteless and very macho joke. "Ugh."

"Sorry. Couldn't resist." He lifted his glass. "Here's to our success. May the baby be healthy and pretty as her mother if it's a girl, and if it's a boy outrageously masculine like his fah…sperm donor."

She almost spit out the cider. "Who are you, and what have you done with Jon Becker?" She loved seeing this playful side of him, hadn't seen it nearly enough during their five-year acquaintance.

"I've got to admit, I'm really jazzed about this successful kid experiment of ours." He reached out and patted her waist.

The gesture sent an electrical jolt through her stomach. She couldn't look into his bright gaze so she glanced over his shoulder, down the wall, directly into his bedroom. Wrong move. More minimalism smacked her between the eyes. That and an inviting king-size bed neatly made with a warm brown duvet on display by recessed lighting. A prurient image popped into her mind. She blamed it on hormones and quickly glanced away, then sipped more cider to avoid his stare.

"You have no idea how ecstatic I am," she said.

He took her by the arm and guided her back to the living room section of the loft.

She sat on the chrome-and-cushioned navy-blue couch, placed her cider flute on the glass-and-brushed-nickel coffee table and admired a small peacock sculpture next to three oversize art books—another fanciful surprise about Jon. The contrast with the "man" furniture was a breath of fresh air.

"So tell me," he said. "I'm all ears."

She felt coy and girlish as her cheeks grew warm. "Well, you did your part."

He nodded. "That I did. And, might I add, magnificently." There was that teasing, full-of-himself glance again.

She fought the smile tickling the corners of her mouth. "And I did mine."

"Yes, I see how this story is shaping up. Intriguing." He lifted one brow.

"And three weeks later, I missed my period. We did a blood test this morning and sure enough it took!"

"Fantastic. What a team, huh?" he said, looking beyond pleased.

Maybe it was the new rush of hormones, or extreme gratitude, but before she could stop, she'd thrown herself into his arms.

Jon wanted to keep the evening all about René and the pregnancy, but here she was smashed against him, and he knee-jerked a response. He enfolded her and held her close, doing his best to deny the most basic of all reactions between a man and woman. He couldn't let this happen. There was no point.

After all his years in chemistry lab, he knew it took at least two ingredients to react. Him and her. In his case, at this particular moment, *combust* was the word that came to mind.

Did she have a clue what she did to him each

time—twice now but who was counting—she'd flung herself into his arms? It was the dumbest thing he could do to let his guard down, yet he savored the delicate feel of her spine and shoulders, inhaled the shampoo-fresh scent of her hair. He'd missed this part of a relationship.

Casting his misgivings aside, he stopped holding himself back and kissed her head, soon finding the smooth skin of her cheek. Memories of closeness and pleasure flashed in his brain. He hadn't felt her tense or pull back, so he kissed her earlobe. It was warmer than his lips.

She adjusted her head and her mouth was right there for the taking. Any man in his right mind would kiss her, but a gentleman, a colleague and friend, a man who dreaded commitment and dreamed of China and a year away, should ignore that plump lower lip and its upper, perfectly fitted mate.

He ignored the warning, exhaled and dipped his head. Just a taste, that would satisfy this curiosity he'd harbored for the past month. How did it feel to kiss René Munroe?

Moist and warm, and open, her lips pressed

against his, so soft, so inviting. He meant to restrain himself, but the lure of her lips made him quickly forget. He covered her mouth and flicked his tongue over the smooth surface, felt the tip of her tongue and explored it. She tasted like sweet cider, but so much better. He drew back and kissed her from another angle, finding the same sweet invitation. Again and again they joined mouths, deepened, flicked and swirled tongues. His body, with a mind of its own, shifted toward her in a desperate attempt to make as much contact as possible. One arm held her close, as the other grazed her butter-soft skin.

One long crimson polished finger touched his chin and slid down his throat, dipping below his collar. Hell, at this point she could pinch him and that would turn him on, too, but that finger and the sensual trip down his neck made him groan. He weaved his hands through her hair and deepened the kiss, then followed the curve of her arms and hips, moved inward and cupped her full and pliant breasts.

Wrong move. Her head snapped free from the kiss. She closed her eyes, though he'd seen the bright blaze within them before she did, and pulled away from him.

"Oh, my God. What have we done?" she whispered.

He ignored the stirring in his gut, and acted as surprised as she did. He needed to do something, to lighten the mood, to distract them from the trail they'd foolishly embarked on. "Hold on. Hold on. We can pretend this never happened." *Like hell he could.* "Blast that sparkling cider. It does it to me every time."

His clumsy attempt at humor helped them both save face, but he needed to say more. This attraction wasn't in the contract, but damn he'd wished they'd taken time to explore other avenues for her to get pregnant. Like the tried-and-true natural way, the way they could easily fall into bed if his better senses didn't keep cropping up. He knew where that would lead—to something he could never give.

He'd already let her down. He dropped his head and glanced first at his feet, then at her. "I'm sorry if I took advantage of the opportunity."

She screwed up her face. "Jon, I threw myself at you."

"But that was out of happiness, and I went right into sexual mode…"

"Stop."

His gaze flew to hers. She offered a measured look. "I think now we're both aware of something we hadn't bargained on. At least, I hadn't," she said, pushing the thick hair he'd mussed out of her face.

He nodded. "I've got to tell you, it's pretty damn strong on this side of the couch." He crossed his foot over his knee, knowing he couldn't possibly hide the full body reaction she'd caused.

"You didn't sign a contract for a girlfriend and a baby."

"You've got a point there. We can't ignore that you're going to have a baby."

"Taking a risk to explore this—" her hand swam back and forth, gesturing to him and her several times "—this *thing* between us is too risky. Unfortunately, our timing is off."

"Story of my life." He went for humor again, a

sorry attempt to lighten the heightening confusion and his drooping spirits.

Her caramel gaze drifted demurely to her lap and her hands. "You don't want anyone to know you're the father."

"Right."

"And you're planning that sabbatical."

"Right again. And you wanted a baby without any strings attached. And the last thing I ever want again is commitment. Any commitment."

"Right. So we've got to go back to how it was before—" she glanced at him and quickly at the floor "—before we realized…"

"That we turn each other on." He finished the sentence for her, used the words he wanted her to hear, not her beat-around-the-bush, let's-make-this-all-go-away-nicely explanation.

She sighed. "Yes."

At least she'd admitted it. He'd have to settle for that crumb when the whole cake sat right before him, fresh baked and ready to… Okay that was another poor analogy, but damn it, it was exactly how he felt. He'd take her in a New York minute, ravish her, have her naked and on his bed before she realized what a great lover he was, and before he could stop himself from making a huge mistake. His ironic laugh tossed him quickly out of the fantasy. He scrubbed his face. "Yeah, okay, well, what do we do now?"

She stood, looking solemn and at least half as perplexed as he felt. "We stick with the plan. We're colleagues. We work together. And you've done an incredibly wonderful favor for me."

Jon heard the resolve in her voice, but her body language wasn't nearly as certain. He watched her fidget with her hair and look everywhere but into his eyes, then came to the only logical conclusion—anything between them was impossible, out of the question, not going to happen.

So that was how it would be.

CHAPTER SIX

THE next morning, Jon steered clear of the clinic lounge. He wasn't ready to see René again after last night. One kiss had led right to insomnia, tossing and pulling sheets, adjusting and readjusting the pillow and cursing like a horny college kid.

He thumbed through his latest journal, waiting for his nurse to put his next patient in the exam room. He never wanted to go through the turmoil of a relationship again. Cherie's surprise departure had left him emotionally drained, and with nothing left to give. Maybe that's why he'd signed on to a sure thing—make baby, stay out of the picture. Hmm, write that down. Exclamation point!

So why the hell had he kissed René?

True, if life made sense it wouldn't be nearly as interesting, but the crazy logic of needing to stay aloof and disengaged from a woman who was carrying a child he'd helped make nearly made his head explode. He wasn't able to say "carrying *his* child." No. The connotations that went along with that would surely do him in. And besides, he'd been absolved of the duty, and rightfully so, what with his future plans. He had to keep the proper frame of mind about the situation. He'd signed on to the project, and…it had been a success. *On the first shot.* He couldn't help puffing out his chest as a macho, top-of-the-world feeling rustled through him.

Stop it. He couldn't allow the prideful thoughts to mix him up any more than he already was. It was a favor. They had a contract. She wanted a baby of her own, and he had plans for a year's sabbatical. Theirs was a business relationship, nothing more. Write that down!

Turned out the fallout was a bitch, though, and he had the filled journals to prove it.

René had made her hospital rounds before her scheduled surgery that morning. It was almost 1:30 p.m. before she made it in to the MidCoast

Medical clinic for her afternoon appointments, and she was grateful for the busy and distracting morning. The last thing she could handle was seeing Jon.

She parked in the back and entered through the porch, a continuation from the wraparound porch at the front of the clinic. Several terra-cotta flowerpots burst with color and lined the picket railing. She inhaled the winter scent of pine tree and reached for the chilly glass doorknob.

The redone hardwood floors throughout the hallway sparkled with care. Jason had spared no cost when it came time to refurbishing this grand old house, and she never grew tired of admiring it.

"Ah, you're just in time for lunch," Jon said, looking chagrined, as she pushed through the door in the kitchen.

How had this happened? Normally he was already seeing his afternoon panel of patients by this time. So much for avoiding him.

"What are you doing here?"

"Morning clinic ran late when I had to admit one of my patients into the hospital for an EPS study." He spoke in between popping potato chips into his mouth. "Young kid. Basketball player. Passed out at a game. Got zapped with an AED."

"Wow. That's not good."

"Good news is he survived, and after we figure out what sets off his arrhythmia, we'll know how to treat it and keep him alive."

She nodded. Even now, desperately trying to stay out of his way, she was glad to see him. He looked sharp in a mint-green button-up shirt and tie with some sort of hieroglyphics on it, no doubt spelling out the meaning of life or something equally as important. His trousers fit him impeccably, and she couldn't help but have a quickie flashback to the day she'd seen him stripped down and jogging. And the way he kissed.

This line of thinking had to stop.

René plopped into a chair and put her feet up on another. She'd stayed awake half the night thinking about the irony of asking a man to help her get pregnant, then, after the fact, realizing she was attracted to him. She'd live with her decision, though. Had to.

"What held you up?" he said.

"I was in surgery all morning. My tubal ligation clinic. Two of the women were younger than me and they've already met their personal baby quotas, and wanted to make sure they didn't have any more." She glanced over her shoulder to make sure no one else was around. "And here I am just starting out. Ironic, huh?"

She fiddled with the single braid she always wore on surgery days and happened to pass glances with Jon. He nodded. She'd made the mistake of pondering her circumstances in front of him. He was bound to comment.

"You smell like chocolate," he said, ignoring the irony and throwing her a curve. "What's got you stressed?"

Like he didn't know. And from the looks of the dark circles under his eyes, he didn't get such a great night's sleep, either.

"What do chocolate and stress have to do with each other?" She'd play dumb.

"I've seen you go for that chocolate stash in your purse when you're under pressure."

She blurted a laugh. "Guilty as charged, but

this time it was more out of necessity. My blood sugar took a dive after being in the O.R. all morning, and I forgot to bring any lunch."

"Here," he said. "Have half of my sandwich." He pushed a portion of a sub sandwich loaded with deli meats and vegetables under her nose. "You need to eat, now that you're…"

"Jon, you don't have to look out for me." Though the sandwich did smell delicious and her taste buds had already gone on standby.

"Someone's got to do it." He flashed a smart-ass smile, the kind that made his eyes crinkle at the corners. "Take it. It's loaded with those dill pickle slices you love."

How could she refuse?

Ravenous, she took a huge bite, then said muffled thanks while dabbing at some mustard at the corner of her mouth.

He watched her with a quiet inward expression. "I like watching you enjoy your food." He smiled again.

Then as if he'd only meant to think it and not say it out loud, his gaze darted away.

"We're not going there, remember?" she said.

"Yup." He finished the last of his half of the sandwich and rose to leave.

A bittersweet pang made it hard to swallow. He was the smartest guy in the room—any room— and he always acted the humble and perfectly mannered doctor. Even now.

Her decision had already blurred the lines of their working together, and they both felt completely awkward about it. Unfortunately, that was the way they'd have to handle their business association—all manners and etiquette.

No matter how unsatisfying that approach would be.

Two weeks later, word of René's pregnancy had obviously gotten out when one afternoon Jon witnessed every female in the clinic circling her, fawning and gushing with well wishes. "Oh, congratulations!" "I'm so excited for you." "When's the big day?" What he didn't hear was, "Who is the father?" And for that, he thought, ducking his head and making a U-turn, he was grateful.

René proudly stood in the center, beaming, as Jon knew pregnant women often do. His ex-wife seemed to walk on air when she'd first gotten pregnant—that is, until morning sickness kicked in. René held her head high, chin up with pride. She wore a white peasant blouse with a paisley patterned knee-length skirt, and looked so damned pretty he could hardly contain himself. Her exotic almond-shaped eyes sparkled with happiness, and when she glanced at him just before he made his turn, their gazes met and merged for the briefest of moments. He read her gratitude, nodded, and though wanting to make a beeline for his office, he went against his will so as not to come off suspicious acting.

"What's going on?" he asked, hoping his high school thespian days might still serve him well.

"Dr. Munroe is expecting!" Gaby was the first to respond.

"What's she expecting?" He'd go for the lame-and-loving-it facade.

His nurse and two others groaned over his sorry joke. René was the only one gracious enough to smile. If he'd been at arm's length, she probably would have cuffed him.

He drew closer as a rally of mixed emotions

made him stiffen. "When's the due date?" He'd been so busy kissing her the night she'd come to his loft to celebrate, he'd forgotten to ask the most basic questions.

"November," she said softly.

"Hey, that's a great month—that's my daughter Lacy's birthday month, and she's a great kid." Why the sudden onslaught of nerves? Could he overexplain more if he tried? How ironic that this baby would be born in the same month as one of his other children. Other children? Only children. He had no claim on this one. The contract said so.

"From what you've told me, I can only hope my baby will have half the verve of Lacy," she said with a smile, and a subtle knowing look.

Out of the blue, he wanted to hold René, to stroke her hair and run his thumb over her lips. To kiss her, deeper than he had the night they'd almost crossed the line. Did it show on his face?

The nurses had gone quiet. The fact he and René were staring at each other as if everything else on earth had disappeared may have had something to do with it. He knew he had to do something, knew this invisible thread joining them had to be severed. He schooled his expression and finished the last steps to reach her, awkwardly patted her back, and when she reached for a hug, he made sure there was at least a foot worth of air between them. This was the kind of hug coworkers gave each other; he'd seen it countless times, but it bothered him to fake it with René.

"Hey, congratulations. I'm really happy for you. Really."

He knew of all the phony business he'd just pulled off, this was the one true statement. He definitely was happy for her, just didn't know where *he* fit into the picture. Actually, he did know where he fit as far as pictures went, and that would be *out of it*. Completely. Which suited him just fine.

"Thank you," she said, patting his back.

"Hey, it was nothing," he said. *Oops!* He'd taken her superficial thanks and applied it to their personal business.

His nurse, Lois, stared at him with a screwed-up face. "You are such a dork. You didn't have anything to do with the doctor's baby!" she snorted.

Oh, if she only knew…

Grateful Lois had saved his slipup, he cleared his throat and made a self-effacing smile, striving for the absentminded professor effect. "You know what I mean." His eyes never left René's, and now her cheeks were tinted peach, which was very becoming with her light olive-toned skin. She nodded her understanding, and he turned and headed back for his office, feeling moisture under his arms, and a grimace on his face.

If this was the way things were going to be at the clinic now that the pregnancy was out in the open, he wasn't sure he'd survive.

The next week, Jon arrived at work later than usual. The early April morning had been bright and clear after a string of rainy days, and he'd made up for it with a long, solid run. After ten miles, showered and feeling like a new man, he strode through the clinic toward his office when he overheard the distinct sounds of someone heaving. The sound came from the forgotten, sequestered bathroom in the far corner of the ground floor. He paused and verified that someone was definitely losing their breakfast, and rather than risk also getting queasy merely from the sound effects, he pushed on.

A few minutes later, René emerged from the tiny bathroom. She tried to slink by Jon's office, but failed.

"You okay?" he called out, brows raised, eyes dark with concern.

She self-consciously ran the back side of her hand across her mouth, and stopped at his door. "That hormone surge really messes up the system."

"Tell me about it. I used to puke right along with Cherie."

He could always manage to get a smile out of her, even after she'd thrown up for fifteen minutes straight. "I'm interviewing doulas today."

"What's that?"

"They're people who take care of the pregnant woman. They offer physical and moral support. Sort of like a preggers woman's girl Friday."

"I see," he said, wearing an expression that gave the distinct impression he hadn't a clue what she was talking about.

"Since I'm going through this alone—" she purposely avoided his pointed stare "—I thought I'd hire one earlier than necessary for the extra help."

"Sounds wise."

She couldn't read the look in his eyes, but speculated there might be a twinge of regret. Was he sorry he'd donated the sperm? She hoped not. "This is the first time in my life I've felt complete." She glanced at Jon. *Well, almost complete.*

He'd paused behind his desk, and she suspected the significance of what she'd just said had sunk in. "I'm really glad to know that," he said, an earnest expression on his face.

They spent more time than necessary gazing at each other, searching each other's eyes, which got awkward. She needed to make her feet move, to start her day, before the next wave of nausea swept through.

"I better get back to my clinic," she said, looking down the hall.

"René?"

"Hmm?"

"If there's ever anything you need, don't hesitate

to get in touch. Remember, I've got superfriend status now."

The damn hormones stretched her emotions as if rubber bands, and Jon's simple offer made the room blur. "Thanks," she said, as she made a swift getaway. She couldn't let him see her cry; he might think she wasn't happy, and she was. "I really am happy about being pregnant."

"Good. And for the record, I never thought you weren't."

She was; she was happy. It was the alone part that kept stumbling her up.

She rushed into her office and closed the door. What was the matter with her? She'd been going back and forth between throwing up and crying for two weeks now. She knew pregnancy wouldn't be easy, but being an obstetrician, somehow she thought it might feel more clinical for her. She couldn't have been more wrong. Being pregnant ran the gamut from elation to hysteria, exhilaration to total exhaustion, confidence to near panic over the thought of raising a child. Alone. There was that word again.

She collapsed into her desk chair, resting her

head on the back. Tears leaked from the corners of her eyes. She swiped them away, refusing to slip into another crying spell. Here she was carrying a baby, two beings sharing one body, her body, yet she'd never felt more alone in her life.

Week sixteen of the pregnancy, mid-June

Gretchen Lingstrom, Stephanie Ingram's doula, was her choice after several interviews, and Gretchen had already given her homework. René lay on her bed reading at midnight, refusing to rest on her clinical laurels. Determined to experience the pregnancy as a future mother and not a doctor, she dutifully perused the pages of *The Natural Way to a Successful Pregnancy and Delivery.* Gretchen's special mix of essential oils brewed on the bedside table, and though she would have preferred human company, the scent offered her a degree of comfort.

It had been a long day, and she was tired. At least she wasn't throwing up anymore now that she'd made it through the first trimester. She stretched out on her bed; the pillows looked so inviting. With hands behind her head, she allowed her mind to drift to fanciful thoughts about decorating the second bedroom as a nursery. What colors would she use? What style of crib? Would she keep a bassinet in her bedroom? And for how long?

Something odd happened. A vague flutter south of her navel stole one hundred percent of her attention. As if a large butterfly were trapped beneath her abdomen, she felt the first movement of life in her uterus. Her hand flew to her stomach. "Quickening," she reverently whispered the medical term for what she'd just felt.

She held perfectly still so she could savor the magical flapping motion to memorize it forever. Normally a woman didn't feel the first signs of life until eighteen to twenty weeks, but she'd noticed her obstetric training had made her profoundly aware of her body and each stage of the pregnancy, and this was no exception.

She'd had the ultrasounds, knew she was pregnant. Felt it in her tender and growing breasts; saw it in the insidious change in size of her waist, hips and stomach. But nothing could compare to this feeling, this affirmation of life. Warmth bubbled up and over her skin from a depth of emotion she'd never imagined. Riveted in the sensations, she couldn't move. Her eyes prickled and leaked with joy. She grinned and lay still, taking it all in for several more seconds.

René wanted to share the special moment with someone. Her parents were in Nevada, and it was too late to call them. Likewise, any of her girl-friends who had young families themselves would already be asleep. Though Gretchen had told her she could call day or night, the only person she really wanted to talk to right now surprised her. Jon.

He'd kept his distance over the past month, and she'd missed him. But hadn't he been the one to insist on superfriend status?

She reached for the phone and punched in the numbers. On the second ring a husky voice answered.

"Did I wake you?" she asked, knowing full well she probably had.

"No! I was reading and must have dozed off,"

Jon said, and she was grateful he knew who she was without asking.

She liked how he sounded and imagined him on his navy-blue sofa, cardiology journal opened on his chest, hands folded over it, feet crossed at the ankles on the coffee table, goosenecked lamp positioned just so over his shoulder.

"Is everything okay?" he asked.

"I'm fine. Beyond fine. I just felt the baby move for the first time."

"You did?"

She heard the genuine interest in his voice. "I did." She smiled so wide her lips felt as if they might split. "Just now. It was the strangest sensation. I loved it."

"Wait until that little one gets bigger and starts kicking—you won't be nearly as amused." A smoky laugh rumbled from his chest. She liked it.

"We'll see."

"We will?"

"Figure of speech," she said. He'd signed a contract releasing him of any duty to the child. She knew it. He knew it. So why had she called him?

"I've missed you," he said, honey-warm tones in his voice.

She held her breath, hoped he wouldn't notice how eager she was to answer. "I've missed you, too."

"What are we going to do about it?"

Wishing she could say anything but what she knew she had to, she cleared her throat. "Nothing, Jon. We made our deal, now we have to stick to it."

"Ah, our pact with the devil," he said.

What could she say?

After a brief silence, rather than hang up on her, he changed the subject, brought up how he'd overheard his nurses discussing who the father of the baby might be, and as she vocalized her protest, they conversed like old friends hooking back up after a vacation. They quickly moved on to other topics, and skirted the reality of their situation—that she carried his child and he was going to China—and managed to talk on and on.

And on…

René squinted and peeked from under her lid. The bedroom light was still on, glaring in her face. She glanced at the clock; it was two in the morning. She clutched at the phone on her chest and moved it back to her ear. Instead of the *beep-beep-beep* of the disengaged line she'd expected, she heard soft, deep breathing through the receiver. She hadn't fallen asleep on the phone since junior high school. And sweet Jon hadn't hung up, either.

After a murmured snore, Jon swallowed. She smiled with a distinct picture in her mind of a guy with tousled hair and a sexy shadow beard. What would it be like to wake up next to him?

"Jon? Jon? Wake up."

"Huh?"

He yawned and obviously stretched. Did he have a clue where he was and who he was still on the phone with?

"Good night, Jon."

"Love you," he said, midyawn before he clicked off.

What? Her hand flew to her mouth. Did she

just hear what she thought she'd heard? A chill snaked its way down her spine with the possibility he might actually love her.

Nah. Couldn't be. It was the middle of the night; surely she'd imagined it.

Still, René hung up and relived those two haunting words over and over again, and each time tingles tiptoed over her skin. Until she couldn't bear to indulge in the fantasy anymore, she put on her scientific hat, then rationalized away every possibility: She hadn't heard him correctly; he'd thought he was talking to one of his daughters; he was dreaming; he'd been sleep talking; the poor man was out of it and confused on top of that. At two in the morning any explanation would do, except the one that whispered he'd meant it, the explanation that stirred her hoarded hope and made her tremble inside.

A little part of her, a part she'd buried and kept throwing more dirt on, wanted to believe he'd meant what he'd said. Hoped with all her might he had. Okay, there, she'd admitted it. She weaved fingers through her hair and stared at the ceiling—she wished things could be different with

Jon. This time a cold chill settled in her chest and dug an icy trail to her heart. This had never been part of the plan. Now, besides dealing with her pregnancy, she had to wrestle with the reality that she wanted something more with Jon.

The next morning, when she saw him at work, he nodded and acted as if nothing, absolutely nothing, had changed between them. All right, so he had been more than half-asleep, and didn't recall or have a clue of how he'd ended their phone conversation.

Case closed.

She'd be a big girl and get over it. Though the instantaneous flicker of hope that maybe he'd meant exactly what he'd said, gave her pause. It sent her off to her office wishing she hadn't rushed into this contract with Jon, knowing if she had to choose over again, she'd go right back to Jon Becker to be the father of her child. But for the second chance, she'd make sure her proposition involved the old-fashioned way.

There was no way Jon would be able to continue to work here and remain uninvolved in René's pregnancy. How in hell had he managed to skim over that incredibly important detail when he'd made his decision to be the sperm donor?

Superfriend status, my eye.

He scrubbed his face and leaned against his office door. He had to think of a way around the consequences.

In the meantime, he must avoid René whether he wanted to or not. He'd sneak in the back of the clinic in the morning, eat lunch in his office and sneak out the back door at the end of the day. He'd survived worse, like divorce after seventeen years of marriage when he'd never even suspected his wife was unhappy. He was the last thing in the world René needed, and staying out of her life should be a walk in the park, comparatively.

There was a tapping on his door, and he glanced briefly at his watch. Not quite time for his last patient appointment, but this could be a chance to finish the afternoon clinic early for a change.

He opened the door and found René standing on the other side. She'd pulled her hair back today and wore large silver hoop earrings. If she were any other female colleague, he wouldn't have even noticed. But with her, he had—immediately after noticing the depth of her eyes and the few golden flecks sprinkled judiciously in her irises.

"Can you do a cardiac consultation for me?" she asked, all business.

"What have you got?"

René handed him a heart test strip and he saw several premature ventricular contractions— PVCs—scattered across the six-second, twelve-lead EKG.

"Where is she?"

"In my office," she said, already starting down the hall.

René ran the patient's medical history by him as he followed her to the examination room. "She's eight months pregnant with her fourth child. She's undernourished, her blood pressure is mildly elevated and she states it's always like that. And when I listened to her heart, I thought I heard a third beat in diastole."

A distant picture gathered in his mind, a unique condition that affected one in ten to fifteen thousand deliveries. The patient history had the markings of high-risk pregnancy all over it, one that should have been followed from early gestation, maybe even counseled against long before conception. Why hadn't René consulted him before now?

"By what you're telling me, she could be in peripartal cardiomyopathy. I won't know for sure with the physical exam, but I may need to admit her to hospital to get to the bottom of this. Did she have problems with her other deliveries?"

René slowed as they approached the examination room and glanced toward the floor. "I've never seen her before today. The history is sketchy at best. I don't think her kids are living with her," she said quietly. "When I asked why she waited this long before getting prenatal care, she just shrugged. I was shocked when she told me she was eight months pregnant. I thought she was around five months."

She bore a concerned expression that, the more he learned about the patient, rubbed off on him.

"Is she homeless? How did she get an appointment with you?"

"I do several pro bono appointments a month,

and she said someone told her about me. Honestly? I think she may be involved in sexual services, and most likely lives on the street or in cheap flop motels."

"Not the best circumstances to be pregnant in. If it turns out she does have what I'm suspecting, she'll have to be admitted to the hospital, and we can get social services involved, for both her and the baby's sake," Jon said.

"I had my nurse draw a complete blood panel, and I got samples for STD tests when I examined her." René knocked on the door.

"What about a drug screen?" he asked.

"I thought of that, too." She swung the door open.

Jon glanced at the thirty-something woman, thin as a slip though pregnant, who sat on the examination table.

"This is Chloe Vickers," René said, "and she is eight months pregnant. Today was our first appointment, and I'm concerned about her blood pressure and her heart." She spoke to the patient, as if making sure she understood why the male doctor was in the room. "Dr. Becker is a cardi-ologist."

The woman's cautious gaze darted between them, her pasty skin almost opaque.

Jon produced his top-of-the-line stethoscope, warmed it with the palm of his hand and placed the bell close to the sternum in the birdlike rib cage. He listened intently, first on the right side at the second rib interspace, then he moved the bell to the left. He worked down to the third rib interspace, then to the lower sternal border. He repositioned Chloe on her left side and listened again, then had her sit up and lean forward and he listened to her heart once more from this angle. There was indeed a proto-diastolic gallop present.

Twenty minutes later, after a thorough physical examination of her heart, and additional gathering of medical history, Jon called the local hospital from René's office to arrange for more tests and patient admission. He glanced across the baby collage as he waited for the house on-call doctor to pick up, and worried about the outcome for this mother-to-be.

"I've got a patient for you. Chloe Vickers. She's a thirty-four-year-old female, multiparity, currently at thirty-two weeks' gestation with abnormal EKG and elevated BP. I suspect peripartal cardiomyopathy. I want her on bed rest and sodium restriction for starters. Labs are pending. And if the echocardiogram confirms my predicted diagnosis, we'll need to arrange for cesarean section ASAP."

He glanced at René, who hadn't left his side since she'd brought him in for the consultation. Other than the faint tension lines between her brows, she was the exact opposite of Chloe Vickers. She was fit and the picture of health; her color was creamy light olive with pink cheeks, and there was a spark of life in her deep honey-colored eyes. He tore his gaze away, while hoping René had lots of extra energy today, because Jon suspected she may be doing a last-minute surgical delivery before the day was over.

With the added risk that Chloe might take off if given half a chance, Jon personally arranged for her to be driven to the hospital, met her there and walked her to the office of admissions.

So much for sneaking out of the clinic early today.

The next morning Jon cruised by René's office on his way to discuss his schedule with the receptionist, Gaby. The door was closed. A young woman with bright red hair, a stained-glass-patterned tattoo covering one arm and a brow ring, sat just outside, flipping through a magazine.

Immediately forgetting Gaby, he pushed on to knock on René's door to see how she was doing, and the woman jumped to her feet.

"Sorry, but it's Dr. Munroe's quiet time," she said.

"Pardon?" He must have heard wrong. Since when had René employed a bodyguard?

"She's resting. She had a long night of surgery, and needs extra time with her feet elevated to make up for it."

"And you are?"

"Gretchen. I'm her doula." She extended her hand at the end of her highly decorated arm.

Oh, right, René had told him about hiring a woman as her pregnancy advocate. He shook her hand and made a U-turn. He'd wait until later to quiz René about their patient and how the C-section had gone, and besides, he really did need to talk to Gaby about his schedule.

At noontime, René didn't come into the lunch-room, and even though he'd promised to avoid her as much as possible, he went looking for her. He'd been too busy all morning to call her office, and after seeing the size of Chloe's heart on X-ray, he became really curious about the health of the infant.

With cardiomyopathy of this magnitude in their latest patient, it made sense that the dusky lavender-rose color of her lips had nothing to do with lipstick and everything to do with low oxygen.

He forked several bites of spaghetti and meat sauce before his curiosity got the best of him. He shoved his food aside. Rounding the corner to René's office, determined to get some face time, he came to an abrupt halt. Tattoo lady stood behind René's chair, massaging something into her temples.

"Take several deep breaths," she said, and René did as she was told. "That should help your headache."

This was wrong. Totally wrong. If she needed someone to give her a head and neck massage he could fill that bill. Hell, he could be a lot more creative than smelly cream and deep breaths. He'd distract her with a leisurely afternoon in his bed, working her into a frenzy and satisfying her every need.

Damn, he had to quit thinking this way, because he wasn't doing himself any favors. He'd had to fight off his imagination daily since he'd kissed her, and his resolve was growing weak. He cleared his throat, and Gretchen snapped her head toward him.

René glanced up bearing a sheepish look, and peachy-pink cheeks, the color of the afterglow he'd guarantee her if she'd only jump into his fantasy—a fantasy he shouldn't be having in the first place, remember!

"Hi," she said.

"Hey. It smells like—" he sniffed the sweet aroma "—peppermint?"

"And eucalyptus," Gretchen added. "Perfect for tension headaches—that's what pregnant women suffer from when they don't get enough sleep."

"Ah." He honestly couldn't think of a proper response.

"Gretchen, thanks so much, but I'd like to talk to Jon if you don't mind."

The full-bodied and freckled, where she wasn't tattooed, woman gathered her huge bag of goodies and prepared to leave the room. "Don't forget to take your prenatal vitamins. Here." She set a plastic container in front of René. "This is your lunch. It's perfectly balanced for you and the baby's dietary needs."

He understood women had different perspectives than men on many levels, but had their clinic nurse practitioner, Claire, really recommended this woman to René? And René had hired her? Which part of the equation was he missing?

He folded his arms, leaned against the door and waited for the woman to leave. René slanted him a look filled to the brim with apologies and embarrassment. Once the woman had cleared the door, he took the seat across from René's desk.

"I had no idea she would go this far," she whispered.

He glanced over his shoulder. "She's definitely into her job. I guess that's a good thing."

She shrugged. "She's nice enough. Very caring."

"She could use a hint about knowing when to stop playing bodyguard, though."

René let go a soft laugh. Up close he could easily see the fatigue, and a touch of purple smudged under her eyes.

"How'd the surgery go?"

She sighed. "Rough. It was really rough. Chloe had an incredibly high tolerance for anesthesia, which threatened her baby. I had to work fast, and the poor thing was so tiny due to IUGR. She barely weighed three pounds—at eight months' gestation! Can you believe it?"

"Yikes. It's not surprising about intrauterine growth retardation, because Chloe's heart is a mess, and hasn't been delivering enough oxygen to the fetus. Chances are she'll suffer progressive deterioration of her heart, but there's a slight chance it could go back to normal size. By six months from now we should know if the disease has reversed or not."

"If we can keep track of her," René said, unconsciously rubbing her tiny baby bump.

If he didn't know better, he'd never suspect she was even pregnant, but he'd known the results, and she'd called him at the first sign of life. He'd been flattered that she wanted to share the news with him, then had the audacity to fall asleep on the phone. Yeah, Mr. Exciting—wasn't that what Cherie had always called him?

"As for the baby, well, that's another story," he said.

"Do you suspect brain damage?"

"It's very possible."

"At least her baby's in the NICU and social services will make sure she's taken care of properly," René said.

"Good."

"Let's hope the little one's a fighter."

Jon thought about the baby inside René, hoping it was a real fighter, too. He also thought about

Gretchen and her bag of surprises, and suspected that from now on, René would share all things on the pregnancy front with her. So much for super-friend status. A pang of envy made him stand. He had no right to expect anything more.

"I guess you'd better eat your lunch," he said, slipping out of the room. "And whatever you do, don't forget those vitamins."

He left her quietly laughing. It was the least he could do. Feeling as irritable as a duck in the desert, he thought how things would only get worse as her pregnancy progressed. He wanted to be involved, yet the price he had to pay was too great. And it wasn't fair to René to insinuate himself into her life, only to leave.

"I think I know who the father is," Lois whispered to Gaby near the front desk.

"I'll tell you who I think it is, then you can tell me who you think it is. Maybe we think it's the same person." Gaby's gaze lifted in time to see Jon pass. She quickly guarded her look and pretended to do some work. Lois flashed a glance over her shoulder, displaying similar surprise.

Maybe it was better to leave sooner than later.

He knew three or four doctors in practices who'd expressed an interest in him joining them, but had been too content to ever give it a second thought before. Maybe now was the time to start a job search; that is, if they would also be okay with him going on sabbatical.

CHAPTER SEVEN

Eighteen weeks' gestation, late June

RENÉ lay on the paper-lined exam table as her doctor performed an ultrasound. The ethereal outline of the baby seemed to emerge from what looked like a triangular-shaped dust storm. A perfect profile of an alien child came into view, complete with huge head and torso, tiny hands, feet and turned-up nose. Could anything possibly be wrong with her baby?

She was thirty-six, and she recommended amniocenteses to her patients beginning at age thirty-four to rule out genetic disorders and chromosome abnormalities. In her opinion, this study needed to be done.

Once her doctor established the placement of the baby in her uterus and marked it, her nurse swabbed René's belly with topical disinfectant, then placed a paper sterile field with a whole in the middle over the X marks the spot. Under constant ultrasound guidance to avoid injuring the fetus or placenta, a long needle was inserted into her abdomen. The pinch of entry through the skin was bearable thanks to topical anesthetic, but then came an odd pressure as the needle pierced her uterus and entered the fluid-filled sac surrounding her baby. She wouldn't describe it as painful, but the process of withdrawing the fluid gave an odd pulling sensation as the syringe sucked thirty ml. into its barrel, and that definitely got her attention. Could the minor procedure cause a problem? She knew there was a small risk for miscarriage by having this done, but in her opinion, the greater gamble was not being prepared for a handicapped baby.

Gretchen was quick to be at her side, and René was grateful not to be alone through the procedure. But holding Gretchen's hand left her wanting, and oddly enough she had a brief fantasy about Jon. Why couldn't she get beyond him? In her thoughts, he sat beside her with narrowed eyes watching her every move, as if monitoring her well-being. The fanciful vision of Jon worrying about her gave an added sense of security to the procedure, even if only made-up.

Within a few minutes, everything was over and she was dressed.

"You know the routine," René's OB doctor said. "We'll send the specimen to the special lab where they'll analyze the cells and study the chromosomes. Report any bleeding immediately."

Now all she had to do was wait two long and nerve-racking weeks for the results.

"By the way, do you want to know the sex of the baby?"

René had quickly looked away from this ultrasound, as she had with all the others to avoid seeing anything that might expose the sex. Many of her patients wanted to know the gender in advance, but not her.

"No, thanks," she said, opting for the gift of surprise at the birth.

"What are you going to give Dr. Munroe for the baby shower?" Jon overheard his nurse, Lois, ask Christina, the medical aide, the next day.

"I was hoping to go in with someone so we can get her something really nice."

Jon craned his neck to better hear the conversation.

"Oh, I'd like to do that. Let's decide what we should buy at lunch," Lois said.

"Sounds good. Um, who do you think the father is?"

"There's no telling. A woman like Dr. Munroe could have any man she wanted."

"You think she arranged to get pregnant? She never mentions a boyfriend, and she's getting on in age," Christina said.

"You mean, like a sperm donor, or a wham-bam-thank-you-ma'am?"

Jon had heard enough. He pushed back his chair and strode to the office door. "Ladies? Don't you have work to do?" He thought about making a snide remark about how it wasn't any of their business who the father of René's baby was. He tried to figure out how he might react if he wasn't personally involved. As it was, he felt paranoid, and thought it might seem too obvious if he said what was on his mind, so he gritted his teeth and forced a smile.

"Oh, sorry, Dr. Becker," Lois said. "I'll get your next patient in the room ASAP."

He rubbed his jaw. He hadn't thought about an office baby shower. Now he'd have to come up with a gift for René that wasn't too personal. Something well-built…and functional…like him. Right. That was the last thing she needed. Or wanted.

He smiled, deciding to give René the same thing he'd given Jason and Claire for their son, a top-of-the-line stroller. On a whim, he made up his mind to purchase one with a special and extra feature, and he knew exactly where to buy it, too.

Saturday morning, René indulged herself in a shopping spree. She'd seen her hospitalized patients that morning and told Gretchen, who was beginning to overstep boundaries and get on her nerves, that she preferred to do this alone.

The woman had proved to be a bit overbearing with her ideas and suggestions, and René didn't want a comprehensive rundown of every nursery item that caught her fancy. She just wanted to shop for her baby...in peace.

The Babies, Babies, Babies! store was nestled in an upscale, Mediterranean-styled corner mall on Coast Village Road in nearby Montecito. She stepped into the display room and almost gasped at the assortment. How in the world would she be able to choose which crib, dresser and changing table she wanted with a gazillion sets? Every color, style, size—simple to ornate, over-the-top to understated to trendy—were on hand for the choosing.

She wandered toward the cribs: natural wood, cherry wood, dark wood and white; French country, modern and Scandinavian styled. There were cribs that could break down to become head- and footboards for future toddler beds, cribs big enough to take up the entire second bedroom in her home and cribs for twins and triplets. Everything seemed to have double functions, and for these prices she could see why.

Her head spun at the overabundance of merchandise with too many choices, and wished she'd invited a friend along to help her decide. She glanced across the store at the checkout desk and needed to grab the nearest crib rail for support. Should she hide? Why?

There stood Jon, Saturday casual in jeans and a snug bright green polo shirt he hadn't bothered to tuck in. He produced a card and handed it to the lady.

Funny how the sight of him made her feel a bit giddy these days, especially since he'd been making himself scarce at work. At first she thought it was the hormones messing with her body, but she'd noticed a consistent tingle shower each time she'd seen him since their kiss. Man, he was a good kisser.

She had no right to think about him in that way—there was no purpose in it—yet occasionally her mind would drift to that night at his loft.

He turned just when she'd been remembering their kiss, and must have seen her with quite an expression on her face. His gaze gravitated to her lips, then, as if he'd been caught red-handed in some nefarious deed, he blushed. Full out, all the way to the shells of his ears, he reddened, and it became him.

With piqued interest, she forged her way over to the counter.

He took a few steps toward her, closing the wide gap between them. "What are you doing here?" he asked.

She glanced at her stomach, beneath the blue plaid pin-tuck tunic top. "Shouldn't I be asking that question?"

"A guy doesn't have the right to come here? How sexist, Dr. Munroe."

She laughed. "Fine, you're right. What'd you buy me?"

He pulled in his chin. "You're awfully presumptuous, aren't you?"

"Okay, play dumb. I'll find out eventually. In fact…" She approached the counter, noticed his Saturday-morning didn't-bother-to-shave stubble and felt that tingle buzz all over again. She faced the salesclerk. "May I ask what this gentleman purchased?"

The clerk's eyes widened as her gaze darted toward Jon. He placed his index finger over his lips, and the woman nodded. She gave René a sympathetic smile. "I think since he paid for it, I have to keep my lips sealed. Sorry."

René tossed Jon a glance loaded with attitude. "Okay, I get it. So since you're here, want to help me pick out a crib?"

An hour later, after Jon had proved what fantastic taste he had, she made her purchase and arranged for home delivery the next week. He'd found a well-made yet not overbearing crib that matched the natural woodwork in her Craftsman home. The fact he'd thought about it surprised her, and she'd thanked him profusely for helping her make the decision.

"I'm good at painting, too, in case you're wondering," he said. "Looks like you've got a week to whip that room into shape before the furniture arrives."

"Are you offering?"

"We could negotiate, but only if you'll feed me."

Could they manage to be in a room, alone together, and not make lust-filled fools out of themselves again? She wasn't sure it was worth the risk.

He must have read her mind when he dipped his head and lowered his voice. "I'll be good, I promise."

From where she stood, she could take his statement two different ways, and the first to pop into her mind made her cheeks heat up.

"I'm sure you will," she said, smoothing her hand over her hair. She stared at her feet until the warmth receded, then headed for the exit with Jon hot on her heels.

Just before she'd made it out the door, over in the corner, she spotted a bassinet. A perfect bassinet. White wicker complete with hood. She stopped abruptly, and Jon ran into her.

"Oh, sorry," he said, his chest pushed against her back, hands on her shoulders. "Didn't see your brake lights."

She glanced behind; his chin was eye level. He may not have shaved but he'd definitely showered, and she was close enough to smell his faint cologne, a heady spice scent with a touch of lime. The tingles cascaded from head to shoulders to arms, making her grateful she'd worn long sleeves and he couldn't see her goose bumps. He'd also managed to erase her mind.

"Is this what you were looking at?" He approached the bassinet, a quizzical lift of his brows.

"Yes," she said, finding her voice again. "Isn't it perfect?"

He locked into her gaze. "Perfect," he repeated, though she had the distinct impression he wasn't commenting about the bed. Needing to change the direction of her mind, she focused on the bassinet.

"Oh, my gosh, look. It converts into a rocker." She laughed. "Does everything here have a double function?"

He smiled and mindlessly set the bassinet to rocking.

"I can just imagine the baby in it," she said, slowly lifting her eyes to his. The subtle expression in his velvet brown stare made her hold her breath.

"The baby will arrive before you know it," he said.

A contract worth of unspoken words traveled between them. As long as he was in her life, she'd be reminded of his connection to the child. A signature on paper couldn't rub out the truth— they'd made a baby together. This child would be theirs, though she'd vowed to never include Jon in the upbringing. She'd wanted it that way and he'd demanded it, as he'd be gone in another year.

Yet she longed for his input, like today, when he'd helped her choose the furniture. It had taken what had previously seemed overwhelming, and made it easy, and fun. And under Jon's tutelage, she was sure to enjoy painting her first room. Too bad he'd consented to not have anything to do with this baby, because if today was any indication, they'd be great together.

She'd crave his wisdom on so many topics over the next several years, yet she'd have to walk the fine line of colleague, coworker and friend. She'd always second-guess her decisions and wonder if Jon would handle things differently, if he'd approve of hers. He didn't want any more children. He'd made it clear—he was happy with his daughters and, at forty-two, he looked forward to a different kind of freedom when they went away to college. He had plans to study medicine in China. He'd laid it all out for her the night she'd asked him to be the sperm donor. How clear could it be?

Yes, yes, yes, she'd said, brushing each point away. She'd been so focused on what she'd wanted that she'd overlooked the bigger picture, the one where she and the baby stood in the center, looking on the outside at Jon. The gap that felt empty without him.

The last thing he needed was to start all over again; she knew it as sure as the baby in her womb. And she'd asked enough of him already. She took one more glance into his deep, distancing eyes, and forced her gaze away.

"Yes, my baby will be here before I know it."

Okay, she'd finally read him loud and clear. The bassinet was for her baby. *Her. Baby.*

Jon walked his patient to the small lab located across from René's office, as an excuse to drop off the paint chips. She'd talked about yellow, or peach, or powder blue—something light and airy—the morning they'd chosen the baby furniture. He'd stopped her before she could name any more colors.

Last night he'd dropped by the paint store and found some samples he thought she'd like, and wanted to show them to her this morning. There was Gretchen, fussing with flowers and candles in René's office.

"She's with a patient," she said, in answer to his quizzical, narrowed stare.

"I'll come back later, then," he said.

He almost asked, *Don't you have a job?* but realized this *was* her job, but surely she must have other clients, too. About to pocket the samples, they apparently had caught her attention.

She approached and reached out her hand. "Are those for René?"

So they were on a first-name basis now. He nodded, annoyed that it bothered him what Gretchen called René.

"May I see them? Color in a nursery is very important. Hmm. That's a no. Oh, this? I don't think so. Maybe this one. I'll run them by René later. We're planning to paint the room this week."

Had René changed their plans? They hadn't set up a firm date, but he'd thought tomorrow night would be good. He hoped, once she'd seen the paint chips, and made her choice, he could pick up the paint on his way home from work tonight and get started on the job ASAP.

Under the circumstances, he couldn't very well tell Gretchen his first choice was the pale yellow. Or that it reminded him of Lacy's nursery, and how it had always felt so happy in that room. Yellow was universal for boys or girls, and he wanted to think that the baby would have a bright and cheerful room to grow in. Gretchen was the last person he'd want to know any of that. As far as he was concerned, it was none of her business.

When he got back to his office, confused over the change of plans—plans René had apparently forgotten to share with him—and annoyed as hell that he felt like a blighted boyfriend, he picked up the intercom and dialed her number.

"Hello?"

It was Gretchen. So he hung up.

Twenty weeks' gestation, early July

How many patients would Jon have to tell today they were walking time bombs? First came the forty-year-old guy with an extra hundred pounds on his frame and a lousy family cardiac history, then the sixty-year-old woman who thought she'd had a pinched nerve for weeks until his office EKG showed she'd already suffered a small myocardial infarction, not to mention the thirty-four-year-old woman with a lipid profile so out of whack she was well on her way to becoming human margarine.

What really got to him—the icing on the morning's pitiful patient cake—was telling a twenty-year-old college student that his heart had deteriorated to the point of him needing to be put on a heart transplant list. Days like this came far and few between, but when they did, they zapped him. Mentally. Emotionally. Physically.

He used to gravitate upstairs to Jason's office to shoot the breeze when work got to him, or he'd spend his lunch hour running off the stress, or having a beer with Phil after work, but today, since he hadn't seen much of her lately, and because he missed her, Jon decided to pay René a visit.

He peeked around the waiting room corner to see if Viking guard Gretchen was anywhere nearby. She was nowhere in sight, so he high-tailed it over to René's office.

For a woman who'd previously kept an open-door policy, too often lately he'd found René's door closed. Today was no exception.

"She got her amniocentesis results today," René's nurse, Amy, said, her brows pinched with worry. "She's been in there ever since."

An adrenaline alarm shot through Jon's center. Was the news bad? There was a one to four hundred chance of birth defects with a thirty-six-year-old mother. He knew the stats, but had tried to ignore them for René's sake. Had he made a blunder beyond forgiveness?

A whirlwind of doubts and fears took him by surprise, and he knocked on the door with an unsteady hand. "It's Jon."

"Come in," she said, her voice sounding muffled.

Jon opened the door and found René crying.

CHAPTER EIGHT

"COME in." René squinted out the latest batch of tears, then quickly dabbed beneath her eyes with the tissue before Jon entered her office. She avoided his gaze, first having to push away the stupid fantasy that had confused and set her off crying. *Jon confessed his deep and abiding love for her, then begged her to marry him. She said yes.* A pregnant lady could daydream, couldn't she?

She couldn't fool him; the pained twist of his brows and rush toward her desk proved it.

"Is everything okay?" he asked, hand on her shoulder, squatting beside her chair. *Sure, if daydreams could come true.*

She turned toward him, admiring the empathy spilling from his dark eyes. "I'm fine, just emotional as all get-out these days. Everything sets me off."

"The baby's fine?"

She nodded and smiled. "The amnio is normal, and with all the new movement I'm feeling I'm thinking up a nickname. What do you think about Tumblelina?"

"Is it a girl?" he said, an excited hitch to his voice.

"I opted not to find out. Maybe I'll just go with Tumbler for now."

"Okay. The baby's fine, but you don't seem fine," he said, gazing deeper into her eyes. "What else is going on?"

She sighed. "I fired Gretchen this morning."

Jon blinked, lowered his brows and tilted his head. "So these are tears of joy?" he said with a smirk.

She lightly cuffed his shoulder. "She wasn't that bad."

"Trust me, she was," he said, standing, then sitting on the edge of her desk.

That got another laugh out of her, and she'd forgotten how good it felt, until it occurred to her that the last time she'd laughed had been with Jon. "She was overenthusiastic, maybe a little nearsighted on the boundary thing and, bottom line, I just couldn't see myself going through something as special as childbirth with her."

"So it's a good thing. You should be smiling, not crying." There went his hand on her shoulder again, long fingers lightly massaging away her concerns.

She fought the urge to lean into his touch. "I was supposed to start the classes on labor training in two weeks. I skipped the first several since I know all that stuff, now I'll be conspicuously starting the class late, and without a coach. It's going to be weird. That's all."

Jon hopped to standing, paced around the room. He stopped, hands on hips, and stared at his top-of-the-line running shoes, then clicked his tongue three times, a habit she related to his style of thinking. He turned his head and gave a measured gaze, then tapped his chest and shrugged. "Here's your coach."

"Jon. I can't let you do that." Was it indecision she saw in his eyes?

"I've gone through it twice, and I'm a damn

good coach. If you don't believe me, ask Cherie, if she'll talk to you about me."

With Jon on her side, insisting he could replace her doula, her downtrodden mood shifted to something more lighthearted. Though the gesture was beyond sweet, she couldn't let him go through with it. "Jon, the last thing you want to do is get involved in my birthing classes."

"You're telling me what I think? Trust me, René, you have no idea what I think."

"But…"

"I think I just volunteered to be your answer. Let's have dinner after work tonight and talk more about it." He glanced at his watch. "I've got another patient waiting. I'll pick you up on the way out later."

Before she could protest, and admittedly it came slow because she couldn't think of one reason to, he had his hand on the doorknob. "Let's eat at that Mediterranean alfresco on Cabrillo," he said as he slipped outside.

She glanced back at the amniocentesis results and smiled. The baby was healthy, she'd gotten rid of her nagging doula, and Jon had just insisted he wouldn't let her go through the birth alone. It wasn't exactly like her fantasy, but it had come a lot closer than she'd dared to hope.

Jon closed the door and fought the pang of sadness. René had looked so pitiful. He'd never seen her like that before. Pitiful shouldn't be in the dictionary that described René. Independent. Yes. Competent. Of course. Vulnerable? Never! Perfect. Definitely. That always came to mind when thoughts of the lovely Dr. Munroe breezed through him. It tore at him to see her so unguarded, made him need to do something about it. He couldn't bear to leave her alone in that condition.

A cold wave hit when he reached his office and started to realize the ramifications his volunteering would have. Not only had he volunteered, he'd insisted to be her birth coach. Was he out of his mind? Not really. Turns out René's happiness meant more than any fallout he'd have to deal with, like caring for her when he knew damn well he had no business getting close. He had nothing to offer her long term; maybe this interim gesture would make the inevitable loss less painful.

He shook his head, feeling another secret pact coming on, and barely able to handle the first, he wasn't sure if he was ready for another.

He shuffled through the top drawer of his desk. Where was that journal when he needed it?

Three hours later, at seven o'clock, pleasantly full and definitely tired, René invited Jon in for a quickie peek at the baby furniture.

They'd had effortless and enjoyable conversation all through their Greek-with-an-American-twist dinner. He'd reassured her about his birth-coaching abilities, and altered her attitude about jumping in late with a group of people who'd already bonded. Now she anticipated a great experience with Jon at her side, and it felt good.

She offered him peppermint tea and oatmeal chocolate-chip cookies for dessert back at her house, and he'd said yes before she could finish the sentence.

They had tea, dessert and more casual conversation carefully centered on MidCoast Medical

Clinic. After one final agreement about his being her Bradley birth coach—another secret they agreed to keep from everyone they worked with—he followed her down the hall.

Because she wasn't completely sold on the color choice, tiny butterflies flitted through her stomach at the thought of sharing the baby's room with Jon. Would it pass his approval? To overcompensate, she swung open the door with great flair and switched on the light. "Ta-dah!"

Dead silence, uncomfortably long.

"Purple?" Jon said, an incredulous look on his face as they stood in the nursery.

"Heather. It's called heather, and Gretchen said it's a soothing color for babies." The remnants of her confidence dissolved.

"Maybe girl babies. What if it's a boy?"

"She assured me it's a unisex color."

"Not. So not." He must have spent the weekend with Lacy, and one of her favorite teen phrases had rubbed off on him, because he never said things like that. He shook his head and took a ministroll around the room. "You didn't mention purple when you ran down your list of colors to me."

René kept her smile to herself. Okay, so maybe his reaction wasn't so much about hating the color as it was about being disappointed she'd ignored his suggestions and painted the room with her ex-doula?

"What about bright?" he said. "Simple? Not overpowering? Yellow. Like we talked about."

She'd been on the fence about the final results of Gretchen's shade brainchild. Now that Jon had pointed out the dreadful mistake, she couldn't deny it another second. Suddenly overcome with anxiety about choosing the wrong color and messing up her baby before his or her life began, she ran her hands through her hair. "I hate it. I hate the room this color."

Jon's expression changed from disappointment to concern. "Come here." He pulled her into his arms. "On the bright side, the furniture looks great! And you don't have to leave the walls this way. I'll repaint them for you."

Why did it feel so inviting and comfortable in his arms? She could stay here for hours and hours breathing in his clean, musky scent, enjoying the solid wall of his chest, if he'd let her. "You will?"

He nodded. "Of course it'll take a coat or two of primer first, which will increase my original price from one to two home-cooked meals."

Without giving it a thought, she kissed his cheek. "You're on. Thank you. Oh, thank you."

He went still for a millisecond, then, as if erecting a protective barrier, he held her at arm's length and gave her a playful glance. "Throw in the birth-coach thing, and I'm seeing a whole lot of free meals coming my way."

His smile nearly melted her, but she was stuck two feet away at the end of his firm grasp, definitely out of kissing range, and obviously the way he wanted it.

Note taken, Dr. Becker.

Jon would have liked to stop the clock, savor how René felt in his arms, inhale the rich aroma of her hair and skin, but he knew better. It had been so long since he'd held her like that, and he missed it. Man, he'd missed it. Now, he literally kept her at arm's length, to keep from making another huge mistake.

He'd made a month's worth of plans with René, something else he should have known better than to do. He was playing with fire by pushing his way into her life, knew the cost would be a bitch, but right now, seeing her eyes sparkle and warm to his touch, knowing she was carrying his baby, even if once removed, he threw all good sense out the nursery door.

"So tomorrow after work we'll pick out some paint, and I'll get started. And what day do we start the class?"

"A week from Wednesday," she said.

"Next Wednesday it is, then." He glanced at his watch as an excuse to keep from making a total fool of himself. He couldn't let her see how happy he was about these plans. He had to save face, pretend all he really wanted to do was help her. He was such a liar. "I'd better be going. Let you get your baby sleep."

He knew he shouldn't get excited about spending so much time with her, knew it would hurt both of them down the line. He needed to tell her about the few nibbles on his job search, needed to be up-front about that. She deserved to know he'd started researching airfare to China, and had been in touch with a cardiologist from one of the Beijing universities.

He'd signed on as a sperm donor, but felt the need to make the kid's journey into the world an easier one, even if only by way of support for the mother. All of this was temporary, just until the baby was born.

Even with this logical line of thought, he made a snap decision to ignore all the warnings and live in the moment. He pulled her close, kissed the smooth skin of her forehead and, while he was in the neighborhood, inhaled the sweet shampoo scent that he liked so much in her hair. Before he could sink deeper into trouble, he released her, hightailed it down the hall and let himself out.

Twenty-two weeks' gestation, late July

"Dinner's ready," René called from the door-way.

Jon had moved all the baby furniture to the center of the nursery and carefully covered it with old sheets. He'd placed a huge dropcloth over the hardwood floor and had the paint splatters to prove its worth.

"Be right there," he said.

She'd spent an hour chopping, sautéing and baking their dinner, even mashed some potatoes since she remembered how he'd raved about them once at their clinic potluck.

It seemed strange having a man puttering around in the house while she cooked. It felt good, too good. She couldn't allow herself to get used to it; she'd made her plans and, due to her circumstances, they didn't include a man, just a baby.

She'd laid out the table; he appeared at the dining room door drying his hands with a paper towel, and with a yellow primer smudge on his cheek. "Two walls down, two to go. Mmm. Something smells fantastic."

The tone of his voice, the content expression on his face and the familiar compliment soothed like magical fingers over her concerns. The scene reminded her of cozy times when she was a child and her father came home from work, always appreciative of her mother's dinner efforts.

What would it be like? she mused as she busied herself with a hand towel.

On his best behavior, he pulled out her chair, then sat across from her. She wouldn't be able to dodge his intense stare, and worried he might read her thoughts as he seemed to have a knack for that. It took her a moment or two to empty her mind, relax and enjoy the meal she'd prepared.

As always, he ate with great pleasure. He chewed, smiled and occasionally winked when his mouth was full. Their conversation consisted of discussing pertinent items of business from the clinic before drifting to the more personal.

"Turns out both Amanda and Lacy are going to the Santa Barbara Summer Soiree."

"Really?"

"Amanda's boyfriend's best friend couldn't find a date. Don't tell Lacy I told you that—I'm not sure she even knows. The guy's a nerd like I was in high school, and Amanda pawned her sister off on him. I've been sworn to secrecy, but figure my secret is safe with you." He gave a self-deprecating glance, followed by a smile. "I suspect Lacy couldn't care less who her date is as long as she gets to buy a new dress."

René laughed softly, enjoying his confused fatherly expression. Maybe it was his voice, deep in tone and always a pleasure to listen to, or the rich food, but the baby kicked her in the ribs. She gasped.

"You okay?" he asked.

"Fine. Sometimes when I eat, the baby gets very active. Usually it's because of a glucose rush, but maybe my stomach makes too much noise?"

He laughed, and shoveled more food into his mouth, and she marveled over the simple pleasure and how she enjoyed having a man, this man, around. Somehow, she wanted to get inside his head and figure him out. "How does it feel having a daughter about to graduate and set off for the east coast?"

"Weird. Really weird. I'm taking it one day at a time, and this weekend I've got to go dress shopping with both of them."

"Isn't Cherie going to handle that?"

"She's taking a weekend cruise with her latest boyfriend." If he was supposed to look sad, he didn't—irritated, yes. "Besides, if I'm paying for these dresses, I want to have some input in what they look like, you know?"

"That's only fair." She smiled at what his taste might be. "Things might get intense if you suggest a turtleneck and the girls insist on showing some cleavage."

He nodded, then got quiet and stared at his plate. "I can't figure out where the time went. I still remember bouncing them, one on each knee, and coloring with them." He glanced at her and smiled, crinkling the corners of his eyes. "They used to beg me to color with them, and I thought I'd hate it, but you know what? I loved getting down on the floor with them beside me, getting to smell their hair, and see their sweet faces so close while they concentrated. Amanda always smelled like apple juice, and Lacy used to lick her lips over and over in deep concentration while she scribbled her crayon all over the paper. I worried she'd chap her lips. Silly, huh?" He glanced beyond her shoulder at somewhere very distant from the dining table.

Her throat throbbed. "Not silly at all," she said,

as the all-too-frequent tears gathered, clouding her vision. Jon moved toward her, placed his hand on her cheek and thumbed away the overspill.

"In case you're wondering what kind of mother you'll make, I'm here to tell you you'll be fantastic."

She tried to look at him, but was too embarrassed about her leakage and quickly glanced back at her plate. She'd done nothing but cry around him lately, and it had to stop. He removed his hand, and she was sorry, missed the feel of his nearness and warm fingers.

"You're a natural, René. Trust me on that. You'll do fine."

She'd made her bed, now she had to lie in it. What had seemed like the perfect solution for her situation had brought a flood of surprises. She loved sharing a meal with Jon, loved having him around, but he wasn't a part of her life. He couldn't be. He saw his daughters growing and leaving home, and she would never ask him to give up his newfound freedom or travel plans to start all over again as a father. His bitter divorce hadn't helped his attitude toward trusting women, either. What would he think if she changed the rules midgame? Wasn't that exactly what his wife had done? No. She couldn't disrupt his life any more than Cherie already had.

He'd given her a wonderful gift, and she couldn't abuse his trust.

"Can I ask you a favor?" he said.

Surprised out of her thoughts, she nodded. "Of course."

"Will you come with me on Saturday to help the girls pick out their dresses? You know, as my backup in case they do go for that cleavage look."

"I'd love to."

The room grew thick with longing, and he must have sensed it.

"I'd better get started if I'm going to slap on the rest of the primer tonight. I'll lay down the daisy yellow tomorrow night, if you're going to be around."

"I'll give you a key in case I get called in for a delivery. One of my patients is very close to her due date."

He glanced at her stomach, then into her eyes. "Pregnancy becomes you."

"Thank you," she said softly, thinking that the smudge of paint on his cheek became him, too. Lately, his appeal had grown to such proportions that it would be hard to think of anything she wouldn't find endearing about him.

Amanda watched with interest as René smoothed the pale apricot silk skirt, and adjusted the finely beaded spaghetti straps of her dress.

Jon sat unnoticed in the lone chair in the changing room, as each daughter took turns modeling their choices. He'd nixed several of the racier cuts and flashy styles, but this classic look suited Amanda perfectly.

As preplanned with René, he lifted his brows twice in approval.

"Some strappy silver shoes and long dangly earrings, maybe a matching pendant, as long as it doesn't compete with the beads on the bodice, and you've got yourself a look," René said, as if a fashion guru.

Amanda's shoulders relaxed and she twirled one last time for Jon.

"I like it. How much is it," he said.

René furrowed her brow. "You said money was no object."

"Yeah," Lacy chimed in, drifting closer to René in solidarity, knowing full well how much he'd already laid out for her dress.

He'd talked Lacy out of a cross between gothic and chic with the excuse that black was not a summer color. She'd settled on a sea-blue halter dress with a plunging back instead of front. René had promised to do her hair and loan her the perfect necklace and earrings. Now, it was Amanda's turn.

"Okay," he said. "We'll take it."

Amanda flashed him a sweetly pleased glance and he smiled at her. "You look beautiful. Both of you. I can't believe my little girls have grown up."

"Aw, Dad, can we skip the sob story just this once?" Lacy said.

He laughed, and noticed a look of admiration on René's face. She blinked when she caught on he was watching her.

"Let's get you out of this dress, Amanda, before he changes his mind!" She scooted his oldest daughter back into the changing room as Lacy snuggled on his lap.

"Dad, I really like René. I wish you could find someone like her."

"I'm not looking for anyone, kitten, you know that."

"So you say. Still, I worry about you being all alone, especially when I move to Hawaii."

"Worry all you want, but I'm counting down the days until I'll be a free man again."

Lacy giggled and lightly cuffed his chest. "Not. So not."

Okay, she knew him through and through, and though he professed to want to be a free man again, the thought of his daughters being on opposite ends of the States nearly made him break into a sweat. He'd deal with it when needed. Not today. Not when he'd just seen two of the prettiest young ladies in Santa Barbara buy their favorite dresses.

"It's so exciting how René's going to have a baby on her own."

"Don't go getting any ideas, young lady."

"Of course not! I've got plans."

Amanda and René stepped out of the dressing room, Amanda draping the dress over her arm. "We're ready."

Lacy sprung from Jon's lap and grabbed the hanger with her gown and, as she passed René, stopped. "If you ever need it, I'd love to babysit for you."

"That would be great, Lacy. I'll definitely take you up on that offer."

"If I weren't going away to school, I'd offer, too," Amanda parroted the sentiment.

His girls never offered to do anything they didn't want to. René, with little effort, had managed to make a big impression on them. But what was surprising about that?

Twenty-six weeks' gestation, late August

Normally, August was a hot, dry month, and the third week of the partner-coached birth class was right on the money temperature wise. The sight of René answering the door in a long brown-with-white-batik-pattern sundress, a motif that looked suspiciously like a Rorschach test, had Jon reading sexual images into the design before she could even say hello. He kept his primal reaction to himself, and purposely locked eyes with her to help him do it.

This more voluptuous version of René, including protruding stomach, was a sexy sight to behold. It charged the positive and negative energy between them, heating to a simmer his new and constant companion whenever he was around her—lust.

He'd taken notice of the change at work more times than he'd care to count, batted the wicked thoughts out of his head and did his best to think nonsexual thoughts about her. Most days he'd lost the battle. And this extracurricular activity with his "coworker," the woman he'd insisted to help with delivery since he felt responsible for her in a twisted pact-with-the-devil sort of way, proved to be his undoing.

Damn. This coaching business was far harder than he ever imagined. It required getting up close and personal. He'd gritted his teeth through the first two classes, being forced to be near René, yet keep his boundaries. Each week seemed to get worse, drove him to his limits, which seemed far closer than he ever imagined.

Some guys took cold showers; Jon jogged. Lately, he'd jogged so much to keep his mind off of her that he'd lost a few pounds.

Tonight, she'd worn her hair up in a ponytail and the sight of a few loose strands of hair on her delicate neck nearly made him salivate.

It didn't help a bit when the older female instructor kept referring to him as the husband of Dr. Munroe. René had piped in with "birth coach" on the first night, but it didn't seem to register and after the second class they just let it slide. He'd slant her a sideways glance and roll his eyes and pretend it was such a pain to be mislabeled, then she'd smile and blush, and the misunderstanding was all worth it.

He wished he knew what she was thinking. Was she as sorry as he that they'd taken the greatest invention on earth—sex—and turned it into a science project between friends? That they'd scrolled over the best part and had gone right to the big finale, missing all the fun?

Oh, wait. Those would be *his* thoughts.

The instructor was droning on, and he needed

to pay attention, if he was going to be any help at all to René.

He understood the "sleep imitation" stage and "sleep-breathing" technique necessary in early labor. In class, he'd helped René practice, helped her focus inside, and he liked how it gave him an excuse to study her up close. In the medical clinic, he used to sneak peeks at her once in a while when they worked closely together, but had never let himself indulge in her beauty for long. She was totally out of his league.

He liked how her bottom lip curled ever so slightly, and that hint of a cleft on her chin. He'd admired her single dimple for years, but she always concentrated in class, and rarely smiled.

Tonight, her breathing was barely noticeable, and the instructor had the partners sit behind and place their hands on their diaphragms. This required taking her between his thighs and snuggling with her, a position of torture complete with heavenly scents and a serious desire to nuzzle his nose in her hair. His fingers splayed ever so slightly as she practiced sleep-imitation breathing. Okay, it was a cheap shot, but he enjoyed the view of her cleavage from the over-the-shoulder angle, and wondered if she sensed his pulse speed up.

Tonight, the instructor had sent them home with a specific assignment, but he didn't know how to carry it out, unless…

For friends who'd never had to search for conversation, the ride home was painfully quiet. He worried René had picked up on his ramped-up sexual attraction to her, didn't want to make her uncomfortable by it. But my God, even if she wore bottles for glasses, she couldn't miss it.

"How am I supposed to observe you sleeping?" he said, when they reached her front porch.

She laughed softly. "Maybe I can video tape myself?" She opened the door. "You want to come in for some herbal iced tea?"

Why stop the torture here? He wouldn't pass up the opportunity to spend more time with her, even though he thought herbal iced tea was a vile waste of perfectly good water. "Yeah, please. I'm parched from all that practice."

A second bubble-smooth laugh rolled from her tongue; it landed on him and set off yet another reaction. The innocent sound started on his skin, raising the hair, then reached inside and tightened his muscles, the exact opposite of what they'd learned to do in class tonight. But stiffening up was his only defense to keep from mauling her. He was at the edge of his restraint, dangling on the end of the rope, wondering how long he could possibly hold on. Why in the world had he gotten himself involved? Oh, yeah, he'd offered, because he couldn't stand to see her unhappy. Sap. Hopelessly aroused sap.

She looked beautiful. He wanted to touch her, the same way he got to in class tonight when the instructor had them lightly massage each body area that needed to relax for the "letting go" exercise. He swallowed the dry knot in his throat, and instead of touching, he followed her into the kitchen and leaned against the door frame, safely across the room.

She moved fluidly about the kitchen in that damn sexy sundress. It swayed and folded around her hips, and before he knew it, he'd lost control of his tongue.

"You know what my favorite part of the class was?"

She tossed him an inquisitive over-the-shoulder glance as she got down two tall glasses.

"The letting-go exercise," he said, not caring that his voice had slipped into husky mode.

There'd been a lot of slipping and sliding into a new direction over the past three weeks with René. He'd seen her skin prickle at his touch, heard her soft breaths of relaxation and had the pleasure of sitting close like a real life-partner for two straight hours each week. He hadn't set out to let this intimate shift happen, but it had, and he didn't have a clue how to deal with it. It went against every natural instinct he'd ever had. Don't get involved with business associates. Don't ruin a perfectly good friendship. Never sign contracts and agree to donate sperm!

He'd spent almost a month of Wednesdays with her being called her husband, and knowing she carried a part of him inside her. As wrong as he knew it was, the term had started to feel right.

They'd practiced the birthing techniques to help her relax, which involved constant yet gentle touching. Her soft skin beneath his fingertips had felt like nirvana and nearly had been too much to bear. He couldn't shut off the quiet roar of desire building and cresting even now, and for the first time he dropped the shield, and didn't bother to stop himself.

As she poured tea into the glasses, he moved toward her and, from behind, placed his hands lightly on her arms. Halfheartedly, he quelled the urge to nuzzle her neck with his mouth. His lips hovered licking distance away and he inhaled the same faint scent of strawberry-mango skin cream as he had in class.

"The reason it was my favorite part was because I got to put my hands on you." His voice, heavy with the last threads of restraint, almost cracked when he whispered over her ear. He slid his hands over her baby mound and wondered at the warmth and roundness.

She didn't tense as he worried she might with his wildly overstepping his bounds; rather, she let her head rest on his shoulder and sighed. It felt so damn good to hold her again, to feel her respond to him so naturally. He'd savor this moment, as it might be the only one they shared if she drew the line, stopped him from making a huge mistake.

"The instructor did say you should practice before bed." His gravelly whisper stumbled over the *B* word. He could tell from the angle of her jaw that she smiled.

"I'm not sure all that practice would help me relax," she said quietly.

He was about to spin her around, when she moved voluntarily toward his body. Her arms wrapped around his back, and she nuzzled her cheek against his chest. He loved the feel of the baby pressed safely between them, the feel of her arms drawing him in.

They stood like that for several seconds, getting used to each other in this brand-new way, gently rocking back and forth, caressing, enjoying the feel of each other. They were this odd couple, family-to-be, a choice they'd made based on her wish.

And their future?

He stroked the thick layers of her hair, she lifted

her chin and he claimed her mouth with a breath of a kiss. Tender. Gentle. Warm.

She subtly opened her mouth, and he pressed against the silky moisture of her lips, as the last threads of his self-restraint snapped.

CHAPTER NINE

RIGHT there in her kitchen René was swept up by Jon—and she let him. She loved it when he dug his fingers into her hair and kissed her, crazy with passion. He took charge of her; his hands wandered her arms and across her back as if he'd been waiting for this moment for months. There were no awkward fumbles or insecurity in his demanding kisses; no, his mouth was skilled yet the kisses sincere and she believed each one. She skimmed the muscles of his chest and shoulders with her fingertips, soon wrapping her hands around his neck, drawing him closer and indulging in his taste.

She peeled her lips away only long enough to catch her breath, then quickly dove back in for more of the heady wine that was Jon.

His hands moved to her hips and he pulled her closer, as close as the baby would allow. His palms slipped up her sides, tracing her frame, then gently over her sensitive breasts. He cupped her and, surprised, she moaned contentedly. Under his touch, chills and tingles weaved together on her skin in wheels of pleasure.

This was no ordinary kiss. It was loaded with desire and a pinch of frustration, as if he couldn't get enough of her. To find herself five months pregnant and the object of his arousal turned her on. She longed for more, as her hand slipped under his shirt and hit pay dirt with the warm, smooth skin of his back. She'd seen him with his shirt off, remembered ever since how slim and toned he was. The feel of him was so much better than the mental picture she'd held on to since that day by the beach.

"This is a terrible idea," he said in ragged spurts, his tongue probing and exploring.

"I know," she breathed over his mouth, kissing him back.

"You're pregnant," he said.

She laughed through the kiss. "Really? Wow."

Amusement rumbled through his chest, and he kissed her harder while holding her hips flush with his. If they were naked, he'd be nearly inside her, and the thought made her even moister with anticipation.

She'd routinely counseled her patients on sex during pregnancy. Knew it was safe at this stage, that with all the extra hormones, the experience could even be heightened. Under the confident hands of Jon, she had no doubt how good things would be.

A quick run of her hand over the bulge in his jeans sent her obvious message. Yes. She wanted him. No doubt at all. Couldn't think of anything she'd want more right this minute than Jon inside her.

Jon knew it was a bad idea, beyond bad, out of the question. Yet here he stood at the foot of René's bed, slipping the straps from her breathtaking sundress over her shoulders, being rewarded with the sight of her full breasts, and pregnancy-darkened nipples. The silky feel of her skin was his final undoing. He needed the rest of the dress removed. Now.

"You're beautiful. My God. So beautiful," he

said, sighing over her lips, then delivering a light, quick kiss.

She dipped her head and glanced up at him, as if shy about his seeing her protruding belly. He wanted to reassure her that he didn't care, but the vision of the dress sliding down and over her hips left him speechless. He hoped the look in his eyes told the entire story.

He ripped off his shirt and unzipped his jeans faster than a strike of lightning, then stepped up to her and pulled her almost completely naked body next to his. It felt like heaven with his skin flush to hers, and the warmth they built between them belly to belly. He stroked and caressed her velvetiness, as their deep kisses imitated the motion they'd soon share on her bed.

It was going to happen. There was no turning back. For an instant a slight hesitation registered in René's eyes as they maneuvered toward and reclined on her bed, and she slipped the final garment off and over her feet.

"I guess I should be on top," she said softly, like a shy girl, putting his concerns to rest.

He wanted to growl his answer, but refrained

while he disposed of his briefs in a flash. "Only if you want to," he said, desperately hoping she wouldn't change her mind. She didn't. Her enlarged pupils mesmerized him, inviting him closer, and he obeyed.

"This has been a long time coming. Let's take it slow," he whispered, with a grainy voice, gently moving a lock of hair behind her ear. He kissed her there and smelled the mix of perfume and woman scent, and grew firmer.

They faced each other. He savored every inch of her, the vision tattooed in his brain. Interlocking his fingers with hers, he waited, giving her one last chance to change her mind. She rolled away and turned down the light in answer.

He spooned up behind her, reaping the warmth of her hips and bottom pressed against his erection. When he lifted and smoothed her soft breasts, the warm tips tightened and puckered and he rolled her back toward him so he could kiss them. She responded to every touch, even when he explored her round stomach with its taught skin.

The baby moved and René's eyes brightened with surprise. "The Tumbler," she said.

He smiled with reverence, deferring to the active baby they'd created, waited until it stopped its antics, then immediately kissed her again, needing to have her on top of him, needing to be inside her.

They rolled together, she straddled his hips and the thought about taking his time vanished. He found her heat and pressed at her entrance, then with her help slid inside, soon overtaken by her warmth and moisture, the heavenly feel and fit of her. How could he possibly last with her wrapping him so tight?

"I guess we don't need to worry about birth control," he said, trying to distract from the intensity of sensation sizzling through him with each lift and drop of her hips.

The picture of her on top of him—hands anchored to his shoulders, head dropped back, a sublime expression on her face, pregnancy-enlarged breasts, round, darkened nipples, faint veins tracking her pale skin, and baby mound hovering above his waist as she lifted and dropped against his thrusts—would be forever etched in his mind. Never would he forget this moment.

They fit as if they belonged together, as if for years this day had been scheduled and impatiently waited to happen.

She was the most beautiful sight he'd seen in years, and she drove him to the brink with each roll of her hips. Tension strained in his groin, as he grew firmer and throbbed inside her.

By the expression on her face, he knew he was taking her along with him on this urgent trek for release. He let her take control, set the pace, adding to his pleasure. Guiding her hips, he restrained himself as she lifted and lowered and he thrust into her deepening heat.

Several minutes later all restraint vanished. They found a wild pace, driven by heat and sensation and sweat. The room went dark as he anchored her hips and increased the force. She clamped down over him in climax and her rhythmic massage brought him to release. The intensity nearly catapulted him off the bed.

He wrapped her tight in his arms and they rocked along as the last few spasms rode themselves out. Her damp cheek stuck to his wet chest until he lifted her chin and kissed her. She moaned her approval, then snuggled against his shoulder again, spent.

If he lifted her arm and let go, it would drop like a rag doll, like the instructor had told them to practice for homework.

It turned out his technique for the relaxation "letting go" method had worked far better than anything Dr. Bradley could have ever dreamed up.

René awoke to Jon's kiss on her forehead.

"Goodbye. I need to get a run in before work." He was dressed and leaning over the bed.

She'd slept soundly entangled with his body, sounder than she had in weeks.

She rose up on her elbows and wiped her sleep-heavy eyes, attempting to get a handle on the moment. "So soon? What about breakfast? Maybe I could make something." The last thing she wanted was for Jon to make love and run away.

He sat on the bedside and smiled at her, though

his eyes didn't participate. It unsettled her, as if a warning of her massive mistake.

"That sounds great," he said, "but you know me and running. I've got to do it." He patted her sheet-covered hip and gave an intimate lover's glance. "Thanks for everything." As if he hadn't gotten the point across last night that she totally turned him on, he soul-kissed her. Then left.

That was it?

Last night the same kind of kiss had sent her reeling with desire. Now, it felt more like a slap in the face. The reminder of his lips all over her body was more than she could process compared to this cheap replica send-off kiss.

He'd made love to her a second time during the night, and she was tired, but if he'd invited her to do it again this morning, she would have…until two seconds ago.

A wave of confusion sent her back onto the pillow. If she could sleep a while longer, tune everything out, when she woke up maybe things would make more sense than they did right now.

She rolled onto her stomach and covered her

head, fighting off a cringe. What had she done? She broke into a slick, icy sweat.

She'd taken a huge risk with him last night. She'd given him everything she had in order to show her feelings. Now, he'd literally run away. How stupid of her to lose control. To open up to him. Whether she'd planned it or not, baby step by baby step he'd become a part of her life. And now they'd crossed a forbidden line.

Pain jumbled with heartache and confusion, muddling her thoughts even more. Mindlessly, she rubbed her stomach.

Why did this feel like a repeat of her last breakup? She scraped her teeth over her bottom lip. Was Jon capable of being so heartless? She couldn't allow the insecure thoughts or negativity while she was pregnant. The baby needed peace to grow, not stress, and pursuing a relationship with Jon would only bring pain. She'd do any-thing to guard against a repeat performance.

She flung the pillow across the room and sat at the bedside. No way would she let him see how she'd fallen for him. If he had a clue how she felt, she'd never be able to face him again. And she'd never know if anything further with their relationship was only out of pity. She swallowed the fist-size knot in her throat. After all the promises she'd made about their business deal, the guarantee she'd given him, he'd think she'd tricked him into becoming more than a donor. A boyfriend? A lover? A father?

A cold rock sat on her chest, heavy and aching. She couldn't ignore the pain. She'd made a huge mistake. She closed her eyes tight and rubbed her temples. Breathe. Breathe. The weight of her blunder made it hard to inhale.

A few moments later, having solved nothing, she glanced at the clock. Reality replaced the scrambled thoughts. She had to make hospital rounds on her inpatients before she started her morning clinic. The big mistake would have to be revisited some other time. Right now, she was ever so grateful for the distraction of her job.

"Wrong, wrong, wrong," Jon chanted as he jogged the toughest hill he could find. He'd been thinking with his body, not his brain, when he'd made love to René, and had made the biggest blunder in his life. The problem was he'd spent too much time with her, eaten too many of her meals. He'd let the lines blur between business and pleasure. Okay, that was an understatement, but where the hell was his IQ when he'd needed it? Showing off in his pants, that's where.

How could he make such a mistake?

He'd told her from the start he didn't want to get involved with the baby, that he'd raised his family and didn't need another, that he had plans for a year's sabbatical, and he looked forward to his freedom, but here he was fresh out of her bed and reeling with confusion. The more time he spent with her, he couldn't stay emotionally aloof, and last night, the distance he'd swore he'd keep had disappeared.

Damn it all. The last thing he'd bargained on was developing feelings for René Munroe. She'd painted such a simple picture that night she'd convinced him to share his DNA. He'd bought it, hook, line and sinker.

He wanted to kick something, mostly himself, he was so angry. He punched the air, as if training for a prize fight as he pounded up the steep hill. His lungs burned and were on the verge of bursting for air.

He'd tell her it was one big mistake. Surely she knew it, too. They'd gotten too close in class and later got carried away, and he forgot his promise. He'd beg, grovel if he had to, in order to get her to understand. He had a bad track record where relationships were concerned, and a nasty divorce to prove it. He never wanted to hurt her. Never. But this couldn't be—this thing between them. It was never supposed to happen in the first place. And now, it had to end.

She'd understand. She was a superbright woman, and her goal was to have a baby, not inherit a lover along with it.

He'd talk to her, apologize with all of his heart, tell her he'd fulfilled his duty, then step into the shadows for the rest of her pregnancy. She needed peace during the next few months, not turmoil, and all he'd done was mess everything up.

His thighs gave out; he plunked down on the nearest patch of grass and hung his head between his knees. He spit out the sour taste in his mouth, then rinsed with the bottled water he wore on his waistband. He held the cool bottle against his throbbing forehead.

How could he be a father and in China for a year at the same time?

She'd understand. He was sure of it.

Thanks to a superbusy clinic, Jon snuck through Thursday morning under the radar and, coward that he'd turned into, was grateful. But he couldn't avoid what must be said. He couldn't let René think he was avoiding her. He'd already messed things up enough. At noon, he took a deep breath and knocked on her office door.

Her eyes softened when she first saw him, before an obvious shift to cool and guarded. "Come in," she said, in a measured tone.

He scratched his cheek. "Uh, about last night," he said, after closing the door. She waved him off in a glib manner, and the sting surprised him. "I've really complicated things, haven't I?"

She went still, narrowed her eyes. "Single-handedly? I think I was in that bed, too."

He let go his breath. "The thing is—"

"Jon." She rose and walked up to him, close

enough to feel her breath as she whispered. "The contract is in place. We can step back and think things through, if you'd like."

"Yes," he said a bit too quickly. "Yes, I think that's a good idea."

He thought he saw something flicker in her eyes. Hurt? Disappointment? Before he could explain more she gestured toward her desk. "Now if you don't mind, I've got a stack of paperwork I've got to get done so my patients can get continuity of care when I'm off on maternity leave."

That was it? She'd dismissed him?

"I'm really sorry," he said, "if I've messed things up."

"Not a problem," she said, her usual warmth replaced with a prickly facade. "Really."

Their incredible night of love had been sliced down to a mere "oops" moment. No problem, she'd said. Except it was a problem, a monumental problem. Jon Becker didn't get involved with or make love to a woman unless he cared about her.

He stood there for a few seconds as her tone

shifted from tolerant to get lost, and he knew he'd fouled up even more than he'd imagined.

As Jon left her office a confused ball of tension, he glanced at his watch. If he hurried, he'd have time for another run during lunch.

Friday was René's office baby shower. He'd thought about skipping the party and delivering his gift in person at her house over the upcoming weekend, as another excuse to talk to her privately. He needed to straighten things out between them. But it would be so obvious if he didn't come to the party today. Everyone else would be there.

The medical clinic closed two hours early every other Friday and today was deemed the perfect day to have her baby shower. Claire was in charge and had gone all out, decorating and planning the menu and baking the cake. Jason looked on with pride as she fussed over the finishing touches.

Jason's gaze stumbled on Jon. He gave that knowing man-to-man look. "It's payback time," he said.

"Huh?" Jon's IQ had virtually disappeared since falling for René.

"You know, René hosted the baby shower for Claire, now its payback time."

"Ah." Jon nodded, and swallowed against the permanent dry lump in his throat. "I guess I'd better go get my gift," he said, and disappeared to his office.

An hour and a half later, Jon stood at the outskirts of the ring of office employees who cooed and fawned over René, who was queen for the day.

He'd almost had to sit down and catch his breath when she'd removed her doctor's coat and revealed another, even sexier, sundress beneath. The halter-top cut enhanced her shape, and the bright patchwork pattern of orange, dark pink, gold and brown brought out her olive coloring and made her hair look auburn. To say she was stunning would be an understatement. She blew his mind with beauty, and he was almost certain she'd dressed this way to taunt and get back at him. By the rapid-fire beat of his pulse, she'd achieved her goal with little effort.

He ate his raspberry-filled white cake and did his best to act nonchalant when she chose his huge box to unwrap. Claire gave him a knowing glance, since he'd given her and Jason the same gift. Yeah, it was uncreative but functional, and the medical clinic partners had grown to expect no less of him.

But he'd gone one step further with René. She read his bland card without expression, then swept her thick-lashed eyes over him and thanked him with an undecipherable nod. Her smile was reserved, her beauty riveting.

She tore off the wrapping paper and gasped. "Jon, this is fantastic! Thank you."

From a safe distance across the room, and with a schooled expression, he said, "You're welcome."

He'd given her an all-terrain stroller. René was almost positive there was a message buried somewhere in there, but she'd been known to read into things, and often the results had been disastrous. All-terrain meant the stroller was built for all surfaces, all speeds. The hills and valleys of Santa Barbara could be explored either walking or *running*. He knew she wasn't a jogger, yet here was this special stroller.

She flashed on Jon running behind the stroller, pushing their baby along on his daily run, then stopped cold. She could become addicted to thoughts like those, and after Jon had done everything but run out her door yesterday morning, she couldn't allow one more fanciful thought about Jon Becker to sneak into her mind. It wasn't in the contract.

He'd made it beyond clear that they'd made a mistake and it would never happen again. But he did deserve a personal thank-you. He'd given her a great gift—actually, two great gifts. She patted her pregnant belly. The least she could do was be gracious.

She waited until most of the staff had left. Jason and Claire were packing all of her gifts into the back of their new van and wouldn't let her help, so she took the opportunity to slip down the hall to Jon's office.

He'd nearly broken her heart by taking off so fast the other morning. They'd crossed over the line and blurred the set-in-stone verbiage of her carefully drawn contract when they'd made love. She hadn't been thinking straight since.

He'd been attentive and considerate, an incredible lover, the kind of man that sent a woman dreaming about the future, and a lifetime together. There was no doubt in her mind he'd been as turned on as she'd been, but had it changed his feelings about her, too?

He'd said it had been a mistake, every last bit of it, that they should both know it, and it had cut down to the bone. He'd said as much again yesterday in her office. She'd tried to cover for the heartache, but even now, even after losing sleep hashing and rehashing the status of their relationship, she wasn't so sure he'd meant it. Maybe her foolish and fanciful thoughts had made her blind, but her feelings had changed toward him. She'd fallen in love. It was the last thing she'd planned on happening, but it had. The thought made her knees wobble. How could she keep him from catching on?

On the other hand, how could he change his mind about her if he didn't have a clue how she felt? Around and around she went, not knowing what she'd say when she actually saw him, though knowing full well it was best to keep her change of heart close to her chest.

After all, she needed to protect herself and the baby.

He wasn't at his desk, so she decided to leave him a note of thanks. She found a pen and paper, then noticed his screen saver—a picture of proud papa between two gorgeously dressed young ladies. Those tasteful yet flirty soiree dresses she'd helped pick out must have made him burst with pride when he'd seen his daughters in them.

I'm really looking forward to my freedom, she remembered him often saying.

Regardless of how many hidden messages she imagined in his gift, she couldn't ask him to start all over again as a father. It wasn't in their original deal, no matter how much she wanted him to change his mind. And she couldn't exactly will him into loving her.

A travel brochure on China held a prominent position on his desktop. Oh, God, could she ask him to give up that trip, too?

Her gaze drifted to a letter next to the brochure with a well-known university letterhead logo at the top. *We look forward to meeting you at the job interview on...*

She stared in shock at the first sentence. He really didn't want to be involved with her, not if he was planning to leave the clinic. She'd been such a fool to allow such fanciful thoughts. After the sperm donation, she should never have let him near her again.

Someone cleared his voice. It was Jon, standing in his office doorway. She couldn't let him know how foolish she'd been to fall for him, how completely out of touch she'd gotten with the original plan. She couldn't let him see her heart shatter. She reached somewhere deep inside and found her composure.

"Oh, hi," she said. "I was going to leave you a thank-you note." Could he hear the quaver in her voice?

"I was helping Jason get squared away with all the loot. You really made out today." Did he need to sound so casual?

"I did, didn't I." It was her turn to clear the fullness in her throat. A stealth pang of emptiness struck so hard she could barely breathe, but she couldn't let him know. He must never know her real feelings. "I wanted to tell you how fantastic that all-terrain stroller is. Tumbler and I will get lots of use out of it."

He closed the door and took a few steps toward her, a tentative expression on his face. "I don't want you to get the wrong impression." He searched the corners of the room as if to find the best words, and she got the distinct impression he wanted to let her down easy. Damn him.

His hesitation and avoidance of tackling their problem head-on infuriated her. *Come out with it. Tell me you don't want anything to do with me. Tell me you don't care about me. Don't let me stand here loving you, when you can't return it.* Heat burned the tips of her ears and the room dimmed. Humiliated, all she wanted to do was save face.

"You think you took advantage of me?" She didn't care if his nurses might be around and could hear through his door. Gossip had been running rampant over who the father of her baby was. "I was as much responsible for what happened between us as you were, so don't give yourself so much credit," she said, sounding harsher than she'd meant, but her emotions had taken over. Before she could break down in front of him and let slip that she'd fallen in love, she charged past him and out of the room.

She'd been stupid enough to think he might have feelings for her. He sure could have fooled her by the way they'd made love, but he'd already been planning to change jobs, and hadn't even bothered to mention it during their casual chatter between the bedsheets.

Nothing made sense. Her love. His aloofness. Their lovemaking. His withdrawal ever since. None of it. But right now, the part that hurt the most was that he let her leave his office without so much as a touch.

The next Wednesday night he showed up at her door when she was on her way out. "What are you doing here?" She faltered over the sudden pop of adrenaline circulating through her. To make matters worse, Tumbler jabbed her ribs with an elbow or heel.

"It's Wednesday, the final birthing class, right?" Jon said.

Damn, why did he have to make everything so difficult? She wanted more than anything for things to go back to the way they'd been, but it was impossible. Not with the feelings she'd been carrying around for him since they'd made love. Her initial anger had cooled off a bit, but the disappointment had cut deep and still festered.

"I relieve you of duty," she said, with a huff and a single shoulder shrug. It took everything in her power to act and sound blasé. Her lower lip quivered, so she caught it between her teeth.

"Nonsense. I said I'd be your coach, and I have every intention of fulfilling my promise."

She ignored the hurt expression on his face, focused on the cold phrase, needing desperately to hang on to her anger.

"I'm an independent, modern-day woman. I don't need you. I'll have a nurse help me when I deliver."

"You know as well as I do those L&D nurses have four other patients assigned to them, and you'll wind up going through lots of contractions alone. I'll help you." He made a solid point, but she brushed it off with another shrug. "This is nuts," he said, sounding exasperated and scraping fingers through his hair.

With the last of her resolve she used her strident voice. "Maybe, but it's what I've decided."

"I'm not going to let you give birth—" he stalled for a second; did he stop short of saying *to our baby?* "—alone."

Her mother used to chide her impulses with an old saying, "Be careful what you wish for." Well, she'd gotten exactly what she'd wished for, a baby of her own, and she was ecstatic about it, but the rest of the grief, the falling in love with the sperm-donor part, she could never have imagined. Check another one off for Mom.

Jon frustrated her so much—being everything she could dream of in a partner, yet refusing to commit—she could scream.

"You're driving me crazy, you know that?" she said. "You want to be involved, then you don't want to be involved, then—"

"Ditto on the driving me crazy bit," he said,

grabbing her elbow as if saying the conversation was over. "Now let's go."

"No!" She shrugged free. "And besides, tonight is that stupid last-class party. I'm not going," she said.

"Then why are you holding a tray of canapés?"

She shoved two of them into her mouth. "Becauth I'm pwegnant and alwayth hungwy, thath why!" She slammed the door in his face.

CHAPTER TEN

Thirty-four weeks' gestation, early October

RENÉ sat at her desk. She hadn't bothered to turn on the light. Early afternoon autumn shadows dappled her office walls, causing a bleak effect. Normally she loved the lacy silhouettes dancing like fairies around the room, but today they only emphasized an expanding pit of loneliness. Something vital had gone missing from her life. Jon.

She wished she could say things had gone back to normal after she slammed the door in Jon's face seven weeks ago, but the word *normal* no longer applied.

With chin cupped in palm, elbow anchored on the desk, her eyes darted around the room, deep in thought. As always these days, her other hand rested on her bulging stomach.

She was a soon-to-be single mother, who'd thought for sure she knew what she was doing when she'd succumbed to the lure of wanting a baby on her own. She didn't regret it. Not that part. No, being a parent promised to fulfill her life in ways she couldn't begin to fathom.

The nursery was completely ready with each tiny item of clothing, blankets, sleepers and T-shirts laundered and neatly folded and in their place. Jon had done a wonderful job of painting, the bright yellow walls were far more agreeable than that god-awful purple Gretchen had talked her into. Really, what had she been thinking?

René could ask herself that—what in the world had she been thinking?—about a lot of things. And one major thing in particular—the decision to ask a friend and coworker to be the sperm donor. Jon had been partially right when he'd accused her of wanting a designer baby, but truth was she'd love this kid no matter how things turned out. Smart, average, fat, thin, pretty, plain—none of that mattered. The love she felt inside for this child transpired every superficial characteristic life could throw at her.

In retrospect, yes, she should have stayed with a sperm-donor clinic, but knowing a part of Jon would always be in her life brought her a minute amount of selfish comfort. And she longed for more of it.

She never could have believed how much support he would be. And how empty she'd feel without him. When she'd made her original plans she'd only known Jon as a smart man, one she admired, the kind of man who would have good DNA. Along the way, she'd learned how wonderful he was, how witty, capable, warm and caring he could be. How he appealed to her on so many different levels, and yes, that he was a fantastic lover, too.

But they'd signed a contract; he'd fulfilled his role, and had big plans for his future. She was stuck in love and in limbo.

She hadn't planned on falling in love with him. She'd only planned on having a baby.

Jon had obviously taken her message about staying out of her life to heart and had left her alone since the day of her last birthing class. He'd also taken a couple weeks' vacation in early September to get Amanda situated back east at the university, and, she feared, to interview for that job offer she'd seen on his desk.

When they occasionally ran into each other in the clinic, they were civil but distant, and the loss of his friendship had left a gaping hole in her core. She missed him so much. So far she hadn't found a way to forget him. How could she, carrying his child, feeling it move and grow inside her, knowing it carried his genes and dying to find out what the baby would look like?

René toed off her bronze-colored flats and let go a sigh of relief. She drew circles in the air with her toes, then elevated her feet on the adjacent chair.

When she thought about names, she wanted Jon's input. What was his grandmother's or mother's name? Did he have a favorite guy name? Did he like traditional or modern-sounding names? She stopped herself. The baby belonged to her and her alone. She had a contract stating as much, and he'd agreed to it. So why did it matter what his view on names was? And why couldn't she get that through her hormonally infused head when she'd found out from Claire that his middle name was Evan! She hoped her baby was a girl so she could name her after her mother, Yvonne. But if it were a boy...

After next week, she'd be on maternity leave and wouldn't have to deal with running into him or hearing his voice across the clinic, or noticing how fantastic he looked in his suits with the quirky added touch of sneakers. Or remembering how his hands felt on her body when they'd made love, and making love was exactly what it was, no one could convince her otherwise. They hadn't merely had sex to relieve some feral itch. No. They'd swept each other into the living, feeling truth of the matter; they'd opened up and held nothing back. She knew she'd touched his soul, could feel it when Jon had been inside her and his pearly black eyes delved into hers, and his expression had taken her breath away. He couldn't disguise that "deep into you" stare, and she'd felt it to her trembling core.

Her watch alarm went off. She checked, then silenced, it. Quiet time was over whether she was ready or not. Back on with the shoes. Another sigh and push off from her desk to help her stand. She took inventory of her office with faint silver strands of light fighting off the lengthening afternoon, and losing. The tone paralleled her mood; she shook her head.

She hadn't meant to highjack Jon's plans. He deserved his freedom, his trip to China; he'd talked about it from the beginning. He'd lived up to his part of the bargain, and she needed to step aside to let him live the rest of his life.

Instead of sighing, she let out a quick breath through her nose and chided herself. *You made the rules, kiddo.* So why was she so lonely and so damn mad at him?

In the meantime, she had more patients to see, and her feet ached from carrying all the extra weight around even though she wore natural-fitting shoes for support. She'd started to waddle, and had hit the always-searching-for-comfort-but-never-finding-it stage. When she looked at herself, all she saw was her belly, and lots of it. How could she possibly grow any bigger?

She blew out a breath and her hair lifted from her forehead. September was almost over, and

October traditionally was a hot month in Santa Barbara. Since she was hot all the time now, at this size, how would she get through the coming month?

About to open her next patient chart, her intercom line buzzed.

"Dr. Munroe, it's Gaby. Is it okay if I add on one of your patients this afternoon?"

"I think I can squeeze someone in. Who is it?"

"Lisa Lightner—she's on the phone now," Gaby said.

Lisa was due to deliver her first baby in three weeks, and she'd had a smooth pregnancy up to now. They'd often exchanged pregnant anecdotes with each other, and had developed a special bond because of it.

"What's wrong?"

"She didn't really say, just that she doesn't feel right."

A flashing yellow light blinked in the back of René's mind. Lisa wasn't a complainer or a hypochondriac; if she thought something wasn't right, René knew she should look into it.

"Tell her to come right in, and let Amy know."

Forty-five minutes later, a very pregnant Lisa sat on the exam table making René feel small in comparison.

"What brings you in today, Lisa?"

"I feel like I can't catch my breath." She punctuated her words with shallow gasps.

With her uterus pressing on her diaphragm, René knew it was a common complaint, yet she took her pulse, which was rapid, and listened to her lungs and breath sounds, which were also fast, though her lungs sounded perfectly normal. Her blood pressure was mildly hypotensive, but within her normal range.

"Any chest pain?"

"I wouldn't call it chest pain. I just don't feel right."

"We'll get an EKG to rule anything out. Have you had any unusual leg pain or injury recently?"

Lisa shook her head. From her history, René knew Lisa had never had coagulation problems, but pregnancy could sometimes pull some pretty hairy cats out of the bag.

To be on the safe and thorough side, René examined her patient's lower extremities, and though no varicose veins were present, she did locate one tender area on the back of Lisa's calf beneath a small bruise. "I'm going to order a D-dimer blood test, and if it's positive, we'll do an ultrasound of your leg to rule out deep vein thrombophlebitis."

"What's that got to do with being out of breath?"

René didn't want to scare Lisa, but if she did have DVT, a pulmonary embolism could be the cause of her shortness of breath. There was no way she'd tell her that; though rare, pulmonary embolism was the leading cause of maternal mortality during pregnancy and up to six weeks postpartum.

"It's just a precaution, Lisa. I need to rule out all the possibilities before I make my diagnosis. Your lungs sound normal, no crackles or wheezing, so that's good. Let me have my nurse check your oxygen saturation and do that EKG before you go to the lab. We'll figure this out before you leave today, I promise."

Making a diagnosis of pulmonary embolism in a pregnant woman was a tricky task due to the tests required and concerns about fetal radiation exposure.

"I'd like you to stick around while we wait for your STAT lab results."

Lisa nodded, and René waddled off to see her next patient, but her mind stayed on Lisa. She wanted to discuss the case with Phil, the pulmonary doctor in their practice. After she'd seen the other patient, she called Phil's office, but he wasn't there.

When she inquired where he was, her nurse, Amy, told her it was his morning to do bronchoscopies at the hospital. She knew that. Her memory seemed to have shrunk in direct proportion with the growth of her abdomen. René lifted her phone receiver to call Jason, the family practice guy in the group, then remembered that after Jon had come back from vacation, Jason and Claire had left on theirs.

That left Jon, the person she'd dodged for the past month. The person she was trying her hardest to forget and get over. Patient well-being trumped her personal concerns, so she walked to the back of the mansion-turned-clinic to find him in his office.

He was on his way out, focusing on a report and heading for his closest exam room. "Oh," he said, when he noticed her, his pupils briefly widening, then going back to normal.

"Can I run something by you?" she said, itchy with discomfort and confusion at being so close to him.

"Of course."

She gave him the thumbnail sketch on Lisa. She refused to look into his dark stare and, instead, she noticed the intricate geometrical interlocking pattern on his forest-green tie.

Before she could finish with Lisa's history, Amy rushed up. "It's positive. The D-dimer is positive."

René thanked her. "Have you done the EKG? Oh, and put her on oxygen before you call for medical transportation to the hospital. She needs to go to the E.R. for an ultrasound of her leg and further testing."

"You might want to get a normal saline IV going, too," Jon said.

She and Jon stood in the hall and discussed the tricky situation of diagnostic testing for PE in a pregnant woman. They agreed the best test would be a ventilation perfusion lung scan, and if that proved indeterminate yet the clinical suspicion remained, pulmonary angiography would be a necessary evil. She hated to put both mother and baby at risk, but knew something much worse could happen if they didn't treat a blood clot lodged in the lung. She worried about ordering a test for a pregnant patient that would involve radiation, even though in low quantities, but Jon pointed out the V/Q scan had the least radiation of any other diagnostic tests for PE.

Being able to discuss the medical possibilities with Jon was reassuring and she was grateful to have him here. She'd missed his knowledgeable input, but more importantly, his friendship. Maybe it was time to let him know exactly how she felt. Maybe after all this—

Before she could say a word, the interdepartment alarm went off. "STAT patient assist in first-floor waiting room."

René's pulse spiked to where she could feel it in her temples. A sinking feeling had her praying it wasn't her pregnant patient. She and Jon rushed to the front of the clinic to find Lisa collapsed on the floor with a huddle of people around her.

Jon directed Amy to take over crowd control while he rushed for the crash cart. René went down on her knees beside the patient and felt for her pulse. Lisa was semiconscious, and fighting for air.

"Get some oxygen over here, and call an ambulance. Gaby, call her husband and tell him to meet her at the E.R. Cough for me, Lisa," she said, hoping the exertion might help break up any potential lung clot blocking her breathing. Lisa did as she was told, but with little effort. Once the oxygen mask was in place, René asked her to cough again, and she coughed a little harder.

"I'm afraid I'll wet my pants," Lisa said.

Relief showered over René, and she grinned. If a patient was worried about wetting themselves, they couldn't be too far gone. "You're going to be okay, Lisa. Hang in. We're going to get you to the hospital." Hopefully it was a small clot that would resolve easily with treatment.

Jon and Amy lifted Lisa onto a gurney and they rolled her into the first-floor procedure room.

Jon inserted an IV, and René calibrated the patient weight and started the appropriate amount of heparin via piggyback into the IV. Because the drug didn't cross the placenta, it was the safest anticoagulant to use during pregnancy.

Jon stood by the crash cart with the Ambu bag in readiness, as Amy set up the heart monitor and pulse ox. The patient's vital signs were challenged but stable. And most importantly, her oxygen saturation was within normal limits.

The strain and fear evident in Lisa's eyes tore at René's heart. How would she feel in the same situation? Scared to death! She held Lisa's hands tight and leaned over her. "We're going to get you through this."

"What about my baby?"

"Little Sara's going to be fine. It's you we need to focus on right now." Unlike René, Lisa had insisted on knowing the sex of her baby.

When the ambulance siren ripped through the air, René let go a relieved sigh. "The E.R. will do any tests necessary to rule out pulmonary embolism, and they'll treat you with anticoagulants. We caught it early thanks to your suspicions about something being wrong."

Fifteen minutes later, with the patient in stable but guarded condition and on her way to emergency, René called in her report to the local E.R., only then noticing how shaky her hands were. When she'd finished, she called Lisa's husband on his cell phone to bring him up-to-date. Lisa's support system was in order. Her husband would soon be at her side. This was a luxury she didn't have, by choice, at least in the beginning. Now she wondered how big of a mistake her original and seemingly well-thought-out plans had been. The baby kicked in protest, and she gasped.

Jon rushed to her side. "Everything okay?"

She nodded. "Just a little shook up from all the excitement." Completely aware of his hands on her shoulders, she'd missed him, missed his company and friendship, and wished with all her heart things could be different.

"Let me bring you a cup of tea from the kitchen." In a flash the warmth from his touch disappeared.

"Thank you," she said, enjoying the brief respite in their strained relationship. "I'll meet you there."

She made one last quick phone call, took a deep breath and gathered her shaken wits, then followed him down the hall.

They sat together in the kitchen and sipped the peace-offering tea, and for a fleeting moment René pretended life was as it had been before she'd asked him to help with her pregnancy plan.

"There's something I want to tell you before you hear it anywhere else," he said, shifting in his chair, giving a wary glance.

She held her teacup with both hands, within sipping distance, swept her gaze from the pale honey-colored liquid to the tentative set of his eyes and the deepening crease between them.

"I've decided to take a job with another practice, and I'll be gone before you come back from maternity leave."

Afraid she'd drop the cup, she set it on the table before it could spill. Her throat tensed and her stomach cramped. She carefully schooled her expression, working to shut down the sudden anxiety as it nipped at her composure.

How should she respond? *I'm sorry I've chased you away. I'm sorry I used you, if that's what you think. Please know I never thought of it that way.* But as she stared at a lone crumb on the table, all that came out of her mouth was, "I'll miss you, Jon."

She'd sacrificed their friendship and would have to pay the price. Their contract relieved him of any obligation to their child; he'd only agreed reluctantly to signing it in the first place, and with one major stipulation—that no one would know he was the father.

Rumors and suspicions were flying around the office like unwanted flies. It was only a matter of time before someone put it together. Maybe he should get out before her misguided plan could cast an unbecoming shadow over his spotless reputation.

How could she be disappointed? She'd set every

single stipulation in place. Why should she feel abandoned? He'd never once promised to stick around. She swallowed the surprising words throbbing in her throat—*What about me? Do you care at all?*

"I'll miss you, too," he said.

They sat in strained silence, her unspoken words tensing the air.

A muscle worked in his jaw, as if he had something more to say, but thought better of it. He stood. "Guess I'd better get back to work."

She blinked. That was it? How could she suddenly be so angry at him? She had no right. He wasn't a mind reader. He didn't know how she felt about him. But damn it, she was angry. Furious.

She wanted to hate him for being so casual about upending her life. Why did he have to keep coming around? Why had she let him? Hell, even his daughters liked her. Why couldn't she win him over?

Thanks to Jon she would have a baby of her own. Though she wished with all of her might that things could be different, under no circumstances would she let him back. The pain of losing him once had been enough for a lifetime.

Her mother's famous saying whispered through her mind again—*be careful what you wish for*— and the hair on her arms stood on end.

Two weeks later, on a bright fall morning, Jon walked with Phil Hanson from the clinic parking area. Phil had a smile on his face, and Jon figured that meant he'd had a great date the night before.

"How do you do it, my friend," Jon asked.

"Do what?"

"Survive out there in that sea of women." Jon had felt nothing but icicles whenever he and René were in the same vicinity at the clinic since he'd told her he was changing jobs. He wanted things to be the way they were before, but took responsibility for messing them up. If he could take back that moment of weakness when he signed her contract, rationally believing he could handle it, he would. Yet the crazy contract was what had brought them together like never before. Would he trade their intimacy for the status quo?

He hated the confusion.

"Ah, waxing poetic this morning, I see," Phil said, with a Jack Nicholson smile and sunglasses to match.

If he'd been released in a sea of women, he'd surely be dead, because he could barely survive the effects of one special person. René. She'd talked him into her motherhood plan, and he'd taken things one step too far. Now he'd been relegated to mere office associate, and the whole thing stunk to high heaven.

"Nah, just licking my wounds," Jon said.

Phil's smile took on a whole new dimension, as if they were old military buddies and had been in battle together. "You think I never have to do that? Come on, a man works without a net and he's bound to get hurt."

"What do you mean?"

"Us guys jump into dating with our zippers opened and forget about the consequences. We forget about the Pandora's box of complications that goes along with sex. Once the ladies find out we're really as shallow as they suspected, they dump us. What do we do? We dust ourselves off and jump right back in with someone else. It's a wild ride." He patted Jon on the back, and forked toward his office next to René's. "But it's exciting and well worth the adventure."

Jon stood watching him, wondering if that counted as a heart-to-heart talk between guys. And more importantly, had he learned anything?

Yeah, he'd learned that René deserved someone more exciting than him. Wasn't that what Cherie had opted for after seventeen years?

He glanced in the direction of René's office, but her door was closed. She hadn't arrived at work yet.

He thought about her every single day and hated the fact that he'd fallen for her. She hadn't bargained for that, didn't deserve the extra frustration, and though it had been the toughest thing he'd ever done, he'd stayed out of her way the past couple of weeks like she'd wanted when she'd slammed the door in his face.

They'd signed a contract and he'd honor it.

Damn straight he would.

By midmorning, Jon couldn't help but notice René still wasn't at work. He checked his calendar to see if he'd miscalculated the beginning of her maternity leave. Nope. Not due off for another two weeks.

He strolled out to Gaby, who talked excitedly to René's nurse, Amy. "Did you hear the news?"

"What's up?" he said.

"Dr. Munroe is in labor!"

CHAPTER ELEVEN

Jon raced into the maternity ward, straight to the secretary's desk. He leaned over the counter, catching his breath. After he'd told Gaby to cancel all his appointments for the day, he'd broken a speed limit or two on the drive over. Though he worked closely with this hospital, Labor and Delivery wasn't a regular stop on his rounds.

Fortunately the ward clerk recognized him from when he'd followed up with Chloe Vickers's heart condition.

"I'm looking for René Munroe," he said, breathless and practically vibrating with excitement.

"Hi, Dr. Becker. She's in labor so she's not having visitors."

How should he put this, direct and to the point? "I'm not a visitor, I'm her birth coach."

That got the clerk's attention. From above her computer monitor, her eyes sprung open and she gave him a disbelieving stare, complete with eyebrows nearly meeting hairline. "You're her coach?"

He nodded, putting on an air of authority, while straightening the knot of his tie and catching his breath. "Where is she?"

The clerk pointed him to the room number, and he rushed around the corner. The labor room was surprisingly homey with hardwood floors, an overstuffed chair next to the hospital bed disguised by a bright quilt comforter and soothing pastoral prints framed and hanging on the walls. But she wasn't there. He stepped outside and glanced up in time to see her walking toward him. She pushed an IV pole along the carpeted hall, and was draped in nondescript hospital gowns, one on backward acting like a robe to cover her hind end.

Surprise stopped her midstep when she saw him. "What are you doing here?"

"Reporting for duty. I'm your birth coach."

"No, you're not. I dismissed you, remember?"

He'd play along, but having let her down enough lately, he had no intention of leaving. He pulled on his ear. "It was so obvious that you didn't mean it."

She tossed a glare at the ceiling. "Did so."

He decided to try the tried-and-true distraction method. "Who's helping you?"

"I'm doing fine by myself."

"When did you go into labor?" he said, joining her step for step.

"Last night."

"Why didn't you call me?"

She broke the pace. "Because you're not my coach anymore." Irritation oozed over each word. He knew how edgy labor could make a woman, and chose to ignore it.

"How far dilated are you?"

"None of your business." She resumed the pace.

He took off his jacket, flung it over his shoulder and loosened the knot of his tie. "I'm not leaving."

"Nurse?" she said, to a passing L&D employee in bright pink scrubs and with a blond ponytail halfway down her back. "I don't want him here."

She turned out to be a student nurse, who had

no idea how to handle the situation. "I'll get the charge nurse," she said, looking at a loss and extremely anxious.

Ha, Jon thought, he knew one of the L&D charge nurses. He'd taken care of her father's heart attack last year. If he was lucky it would be her and he'd convince her to let him stay regardless of what René said. In the meantime, he followed her down the corridor.

"Don't make a scene, René. I want to help you."

"Not going to happen." She turned to walk in the other direction.

"Come on, let's go back to your room," he said, reaching for her arm.

She pulled away from his grasp. Grumpy from labor or not, her reaction surprised the hell out of him. He might need to take another approach.

"I'm supposed to keep walking to help speed things along." She shot past him in a new direction.

He strode up behind her. "Then I'll walk with you."

She stopped again, and he almost ran into her. "I want you to leave."

The charge nurse approached. Unfortunately, it wasn't the one he knew. This called for drastic action, and he'd do whatever it took. He flung his arm around René's shoulder. "Come on, honey pie, let's keep walking." He'd play the patient partner to her testy labor lady.

She responded with an alien death glare.

"Is this man bothering you, Dr. Munroe?"

"I don't want him here."

"I'm the birth coach," he said, fighting to keep his hand on her shoulder even as she pinched his fingers. "Her doula. I see the labor has really made her cranky." He smiled and sidestepped when she tried to kick his foot. Fortunately she was only wearing the hospital-issued no-skid sock slippers.

The no-nonsense charge nurse glanced back and forth between them, appraising the situation.

"If you don't believe me, check her paperwork," he said. "My name's Jon Becker, Dr. Jon Becker, and it should be there." They'd filled out the forms together in the first Bradley birthing class. "And while you're at it—" he decided to go for broke in case he got thrown out of the hospital in the next few minutes, and because he wanted to make sure René didn't get dehydrated in his absence "—can you bring her a cup of ice chips?"

René gasped and grabbed her side, standing like a statue as the obvious contraction mounted.

Jon seized the opportunity to take over. "Okay, let me get a wheelchair and I'll take you back to the room." He saw one halfway down the hall and charged toward it. "Don't worry, I'm here and I'll take care of you," he said, rolling it back. "I'll even make the pillows just how you like them."

He had the wheelchair behind her knees before René could say "ouch" and Jon assisted her to sit, then rolled her to the room.

"Don't forget the sleep breathing. Think like an animal, go inward." He used calming low tones to help her stay focused, the way he'd been taught.

The charge nurse must have gone to check the paperwork, because they were alone again, and Jon helped René get into the awaiting bed. She let him.

He whispered encouraging words and rubbed her arm while helping her lay on her side. He put a pillow behind her back, two under her head and one between her knees the way they'd practiced in class, and again, she didn't protest.

He lightly stroked her hair and massaged her neck. Every lesson they'd learned together came back to him, plus a few he'd remembered from the birth of his daughters. He'd be useful to her. He owed her no less.

When her breathing returned to normal, she glanced over her shoulder and whispered a surprising, "Thanks."

"You're not kicking me out?" He smiled tenderly at her, wanting more than anything for her to understand he'd be there if she needed him, as long as she let him.

She shook her head, eyes half-mast. A second later her earnest gaze went directly for his pupils. "The baby's almost four weeks premature. I had a bloody show yesterday after work, then I realized I'd been having irregular contractions most of the afternoon. It's too early—I'm scared."

"Hey, you're in great hands." He reached for her fingers and offered a reassuring squeeze. "This hospital is top-notch. The baby will get all the help she needs."

"She?" she said, with a toss of her thick lashes. "You know something I don't?"

"Actually, with my two-girl track record, just call it a hunch."

The L&D nurse stepped back into the room, ice chips in one hand, monitor wires in the other. She went to work setting up the external device, then did a cervical check. Out of courtesy, Jon looked away while she did.

"You're six centimeters dilated and fifty percent effaced. Looks like we're getting somewhere."

A combination apprehensive and excited smile creased René's lips. Her raised eyebrows cried out for reassurance. He wasn't used to seeing her look insecure, but the pyramid of lines on her forehead and the constant lip licking told him she was. She glanced toward him and he made an encouraging nod.

"Piece of cake, huh?" he said.

"That's easy for you to say." She huffed.

He ducked when she tried to swat him with one of the pillows.

"Things might get ugly," she warned with a flinty look.

"I can take it," he said, giving in to the need to smooth her hair. "Hey, I've got my mp3 player—you want to listen to some music?"

"Sure." She nodded, a whole new attitude to his being there, which buoyed his spirit.

She sat up and he put the ear buds in place, and let her choose whatever she wanted to listen to from his personal list.

She settled back into the pile of pillows. He spoon-fed her a couple of ice chips, treating her like Cleopatra.

"Just do me a favor," she said, around a mouthful of ice.

"Sure, anything."

"Don't ever call me 'honey pie' again."

A laugh tumbled out of his mouth as she gave her warning. He took note. A gaze passed between them, communicating a book's worth of regulations, and maybe forgiveness. For now they'd put all the confusion about where they stood with each other aside and work as a team for one goal, the birth of the baby they'd made together.

Four hours later, during a lull between contractions, René twirled her hair around her index finger. "Tell me something silly about you," she said.

"Me, silly? Man, that's a tough one." After some thought, and under the time constraint of wanting to say something before the next big one came along, he remembered a long-buried factoid. "I used to, probably still do, know all the words to 'Bohemian Rhapsody.'"

She bleated a laugh. "You're kidding. Okay. Tell me."

He'd do anything to smooth the furrow between her brows and ease this ordeal she was going through, and figured what the hell. After a moment of digging through his memory, he recited every single word to the old Queen song.

Her laughter trickled out, and he savored this sound compared to her last contraction and the injured animal echoing in his memory. Thankfully, the nurse had started titrating a mild sedative into her IV to help her relax between contractions, and the result was noticeable.

"Your turn," Jon said, taking advantage of her new and relaxed state.

She looked all innocent, as if the game had changed.

"Come on, I told you mine, now you tell me yours," he chided.

"Okay." She sighed and glanced at the ceiling, a light blush coloring her cheeks. "I used to know all the dance steps to *Thriller*."

"Ha!" He could just imagine René dancing like a zombie, and it cracked him up. "Someday I'm going to make you show me."

The sentence had slipped out with little thought. The consequences sent them spiraling into the reality of their relationship. There would be no someday. Their eyes fused and communicated questions and answers and regrets, though no word was spoken.

"Sure," she said.

After several more seconds of strained silence she shook her head, then grabbed her belly with both hands. "Oh, oh, oh. Tumbler wants out."

"Come on now, breathe." He jumped back to duty, soothing her, helping her find a tolerable position, waiting for the contraction to pass.

The L&D nurse checked in, did another cervical

exam and monitored the baby. The fetal heartbeat had become a mesmerizing rhythm and a reassuring sound in between the contractions. Their little Tumbler was working hard, too, and Jon wouldn't forget that.

"Maybe you should take a break," the nurse said to Jon. "Go eat something. You don't want to run out of steam when the real show starts."

He thought he'd been watching the real show for more than four hours. He'd been holding René's hand, and neither of them seemed to realize how natural it was. She let go and prodded him with a direct look, then a wink. "Go on. Take a break. I'll be fine."

He didn't want to leave her, but the nurse had made a good point. "I'm not hungry, but maybe a quick visit to the men's room and a bottle of water will do me some good."

"Go, go," she said, acting as if she didn't need him.

Once alone, Jon dealt with his torn feelings. It felt so right to be with her, yet he had a job transfer arranged for the end of the month. And China? What about China? Was he here out of a sense of duty or because he cared for her? When he saw their baby, how would he react?

He splashed cold water on his face and washed his hands, avoiding the answers, soon rushing back to her side.

Back within five minutes, she was noticeably glad to see him. He resumed his position at her bedside, touching, massaging, and repositioning her—anything she wanted to make her relax between contractions as the afternoon dragged on into the evening.

Two hours later, drenched in sweat, writhing in midcontraction, René rolled onto her side. Jon rubbed her lower back until he thought his arm would fall off. She clutched his other hand so tight, he'd lost feeling in his fingers.

"You can do this, René. Don't quit."

"I can't. I'm dead."

"Come on, honey. Don't give up."

After the contraction eased up, she got a peculiar expression on her face; a laugh vibrated and rolled out of her chest, taking him by surprise.

"What's so funny?" he asked.

"I'm an OB doc. You'd think I'd know how

horrible labor is. Truth is, the nurses take care of my patients, and I just show up for the grand finale."

"Humbling, eh?"

She gave a self-deprecating glance, then slid into the next contraction with a *"Yeow!"*

After another quick check, the nurse made the call. "Okay, it's time to deliver this baby." She pushed a button on the wall. Then over her shoulder and through the com line, she called the charge nurse. "Page Dr. Stevens. We're ready for a baby to get born."

René looked at Jon with a see-what-I'm-saying lift of her brows.

He grinned. "Are you ready?"

"I changed my mind. Can I check out now?"

He laughed. "I know you can do this, honey, and if I can help in any way I will."

An amused look crossed her face. "I think you already did." It only lasted a second before a grimace appeared, followed by the horrific painful expression only a woman in transition can make.

The doctor arrived and did a quick vaginal examination, determining the position and station of the fetal head. Jon winced.

"Bear down," the doctor said, as the next tsunami contraction rolled through.

Jon was there by her side, holding her hands, prompting her just like the doctor and delivery nurse were. "Push. Push, honey. Come on, baby, you can do it."

His eyes latched on to hers and he could have sworn her look of terror changed to trust. She put her chin to chest, and let go a guttural animal sound and pushed so hard he was afraid she'd have a brain aneurysm.

"We're almost there," the doctor said.

She went limp after the contraction eased off, as if too exhausted to move or breathe. He held her against his chest, wiped her sweat-wrung brow, kissed her head and cuddled her. She felt more precious to him than anything on earth. "You're doing great. You're almost there," he whispered in her ear.

Soon the now-familiar fetal monitor started its earthquake detection and her moan seemed to originate from her toes.

"This is it," the doctor said. "Bear down."

Exhausted, Jon tensed and didn't make a peep when her grip and nails drew blood on his palms. "Push, René. Come on, baby, push. You can do it. We're almost there." His voice was hoarse with fatigue, and he could only imagine how wrung out René must feel.

But she grunted and growled, and pushed and pushed like the trooper she was, and he admired the hell out of her for it. Loved her.

Soon a mewing sound came from the foot of the bed. From Jon's angle a slick and hairless object popped out and slipped into the doctor's awaiting hands.

René cried out in sudden relief. In awe, Jon bit his lip and held his breath. Shivers of joy coursed through him. His blurry gaze melded with her watery amber eyes. He wanted to yell, *We did it!* but couldn't form the words. They smiled, clutching each other's hands, passing volumes of thoughts and feelings between them. How could a single word express the wonder, the elation?

The nurse burst their moment by handing the baby to René, and he became the center of their existence. The reason they'd come together in the first place. The final note of a beautiful symphony.

The tiny body jerked and spasmed and imitated a griping kitten. He and René laughed together with utter joy. Joy that Jon hadn't felt since his daughters had been born.

"It's a boy," the doctor declared.

Chills ran the course of Jon's body as he looked at the baby. A son!

Overwhelmed, he needed to find somewhere to sit down as the blood receded from his head and down to his toes.

"Uh-oh, husband down," the doctor said.

"Lean against the wall and slide down," the nurse directed, busy with the newborn.

Jon found the nearest wall and fought the darkness overtaking his vision. He skid his back down the wall all the way to the floor, then put his head between his knees and snagged a couple of deep breaths. "Sorry, René," he mumbled, as if this had been the only way he'd let her down. A beat later, everything else faded away.

A boy. Their baby was a boy. A small, but healthy boy.

Willing himself not to go completely out, he glanced up in time to see René cuddle new life to her chest. "Oh, God, he's gorgeous," she said, with a grainy, exhausted voice.

Jon closed his eyes. Yes. Yes. They'd done great work, the two of them. Feeling a bit stronger, he took his time standing, and when he was sure he was back to normal, he approached the bed.

"Don't touch him," the nurse said. "Your hands were on the floor."

He pocketed his hands and leaned over René to have a look at the baby. She gazed up at him, eyes glistening, and with a joyous smile stretching her lips. "Thank you," she said, serene and angelic. "I've got my baby."

He wanted to say, *No, thank* you! *Thank you for reminding me what living is, for pulling me out of my cave and forcing me to interact with life and to feel again.* But his thoughts were flying too fast, and he couldn't form a single syllable. Instead, he leaned over and kissed the delicate crease on her brow, savored her warm skin beneath his lips, and when he'd recovered his voice he whispered, "My pleasure. Truly."

Their eyes connected again. Something solid and everlasting passed between them, the sense of family he remembered so well from the birth of both of his daughters. A bond that could never be altered bridged between them, an impermeable connection in the form of a fragile baby joined them heart to heart, whether he wanted it or not.

A sting of panic shot through Jon's center, jolting him back to reality. This wasn't part of the contract. She wanted a baby, not him. He was nothing more than a conduit to her dreams. He had to remember his place, steer clear of the dangerous lure the thought of having a son had brought.

There was no place in René's plan for him.

And he had a life…with plans. He already knew he couldn't work side by side with her, and be uninvolved. Now, with the birth of their son—correction, *her* son—the only thing left was for him to move away. Far away. It was best for all three of them.

From the beginning, she'd made it clear she

wanted this baby all to herself. Hadn't she tried to banish him from the delivery room? He'd bulldozed his way in. This cockamamy baby-plan stunt wasn't how families got formed. Any fleeting thoughts about being a part of their lives were a sham. And no matter what, no matter how much his instinct contradicted his future plans, he was going to China.

He glanced at mother and baby, a near-perfect picture of bliss; still, he ached to be a part of it. Taking to heart the nurse's advice—*don't touch him, don't dare touch him*—he backed away.

As they cleaned up both mother and baby, Jon stood dazed, an outside observer. Finally, the nurse announced she was rolling René back to the ward.

Reeling with confusion, Jon hung back. If she loved him, maybe things could be different, but she'd never hinted at anything close to that, and he'd never had the guts to tell her...

Someone was speaking to him.

"Sorry. What?" he said.

"Spell your last name for the birth certificate." The ward clerk was finishing up the paperwork.

That damn contract waved like the Great Wall of China between them.

"Oh. You've got it wrong," he said. "I'm not the father." How could he ever face himself again after this bold-faced lie? "I'm just the birth coach."

René overhead Jon's faltering voice, heard it crack when he said he wasn't the father, and the euphoria slipped from her grasp. She held her baby close, the precious life she was responsible for, as the point drove hard into her heart—it would just be the two of them. She tried with what little strength she had left not to let the devastating ache in her chest subtract from the most incredible moment of her life. She had a baby. With tears prickling her eyes, she swallowed hard against her reality.

She kissed her son's perfect little head and whispered, "It's just you and me, kid."

CHAPTER TWELVE

Two weeks later

RENÉ finished diapering Evan, and patted his thigh, then pretended to eat his toes. The baby squirmed and stretched, then yawned, obviously bored with her adoration. She grinned and made the final snap on his terry sleeper before swaddling him. Filled to the gills with her breast milk, he was ready for his nap.

She'd seen the dreamy look in the eyes of new mothers, but never, ever could she fathom the depth of emotion and love having a baby could evoke, until now. She mindlessly hummed and savored the intensity of her feelings for Evan. This was how life was meant to be, filled with love and purpose.

She cuddled her boy, sniffed his baby scent and kissed his ever-fattening cheeks, then put him in the bassinet.

A few moments later, she stood in the living room that had been half overtaken by It's a Boy balloons, congratulatory plant baskets and flower arrangements. She looked out the front window at the avocado tree in her yard, while Evan took his second nap of the day.

She should be ecstatic about her small but mighty boy, and no doubt about it she was, but sometimes ladies got a little blue after giving birth and, unfortunately, she'd become one of them. She loathed the constant whispering sadness that subtly eroded her newfound happiness.

As if fresh out of rehab, she only allowed herself to think about Jon once or twice a day.

Jon had stayed by her side throughout the entire labor. Even after she'd acted horribly and banished him, he'd hung around to coach her through the ordeal. She didn't know how she would have made it through without him. Then, when it was over, he'd disappeared.

After they'd cleaned up the baby and announced he'd weighed five pounds, fifteen ounces, and she'd been rolled off to her room, Jon had never shown his face. And since she and Evan had been home, he hadn't called or come by.

His neglect stabbed at her and hurt worse than labor.

And the lingering heartache looped over and over in her brain. *You've got it wrong. I'm not the father,* he'd told the nurse. She'd heard correctly.

He'd given her free rein over the child, just like their contract agreed he would. She'd gotten her wish…and couldn't be more miserable if she tried.

Staring out at the tree, she shook her head, fed up with the blues trailing her everywhere she went. She'd been proactive her entire life, yet now she sat passively back like a hurt and sulking teenager.

Well, she'd had enough of this nonsense. Even if Jon wasn't going to be a part of their lives, he should at least come to see the baby now that his birth-misshapen head had rounded, his umbilical cord had dried and fallen off and his scrawny body had started to fill out. Evan was so beautiful. If Jon saw how the boy looked like him, even at this early stage, how his eyes were dark and intense just like his, maybe he'd think twice about taking that other job or going to China.

If she told him how she really felt, not the part about being livid with him for staying away, but the depth of her love for him that she knew beyond doubt wasn't merely because of gratitude, maybe he'd reconsider.

She'd given him two weeks to mull things over, to come to his senses and accept they were meant to be together. Still, he hadn't come. She didn't want to lose Jon; the thought loomed overhead, sending shivers through her like a cloud of ice. The breath left her lungs too quickly as she worried she may already have lost him.

He needed to know she loved him.

She remembered his smiling face and encouraging comments when she wanted to give up during labor, and how his hands seemed to find the perfect spot to massage when the baby's head pressed on her spine. He'd seen her at her worst. God, did she really say some of those horrible things? After so many hours in labor she must have looked more like a horror movie star than human. And she'd never, ever, admitted to anyone that she knew all the steps to *Thriller!*

She covered her face in her hand and couldn't help but smile along with the grimace. The man knew everything about her. Except that she loved him.

Another anxious pang sent her striding across the room, chewing at her lip.

René didn't know what she would have done without Claire, who'd come by every day since Evan was born. The look of shock on her face when René finally opened up and told Claire who the sperm donor was had been priceless. If she weren't so miserable, she might laugh. Just yesterday, Claire warned that Jon and Jason were actively looking for his replacement at MidCoast Medical, as if she knew more was at stake than just a change in job. René had shuttered her reaction and changed the subject back to the baby rather than let on how the news had quaked through her.

But the news tore at her already-punctured heart, and after Claire had left, she'd cried. She'd sobbed until her ribs ached and her eyes were swollen, and the baby's nursery monitor forced her to put her attention somewhere else. Thank goodness for Evan, for holding her together, for giving her something to live for.

She settled on the couch and stared at her lap and the hands with a noticeably empty ring finger. She'd never even tried to tell Jon her real feelings, and as smart as he was, he wasn't a mind reader.

René made a ragged sigh. She'd had enough wallowing in self-pity. Like the story went, if she wanted change, she have to make it. Standing, she walked to the kitchen, to the wireless phone charging in its cradle, as electrical currents strong enough to light the moon coursed through her. With a trembling hand, she punched in his number. If she didn't at least try, she'd never forgive herself.

It was late enough Saturday morning to know he'd be finished with his run. And, by God, she'd talk to him today, no matter how hard or scary, and find out why he hadn't been by to see their baby.

Or her.

There was no excuse for it, unless he was a coward, and how could she possibly love a coward?

Her shoulders slumped from their militant tension. She was so full of nonsense. The only thing that mattered was the truth. How could he change his mind about leaving if she didn't tell him how she truly felt?

She was in love with him. He deserved to know.

Jon's hand cramped as he finished another page in his journal. How did a man explain to his son why he wouldn't be a part of his life? It seemed he'd been writing everything he wanted the boy to know in life for two straight weeks.

Notes to my son.

Was it even fair to use the word *my* in referring to Evan? He only knew the boy's name, after his middle name, from the women at work. Claire and the other nurses couldn't stop talking about René's new baby. They gossiped openly about who the father might be, suspecting she'd used a donor. Claire had started looking at him different, but maybe he was being paranoid about that.

At the clinic, he'd clenched his jaw so tight so often it had started crackling when he ate. But who was eating? He'd lost his appetite, had turned into an insomniac and had been listless for two weeks.

How many times had he started out the door to go see René and the baby? As many times as he'd turned back.

The phone rang and his pulse sped up when he saw René's name in the caller ID box. As rough as it had been, twisting and ripping at his conscience, he'd kept his word. The baby was hers and hers alone. She needn't worry about that.

"René," he said, disguising the uncertainty. "I was just thinking about you."

"You were?" She sounded surprised, and it sent another pang of guilt through his chest. "I need to talk to you. Will you come to see us?"

Could he handle being near René and seeing Evan? If he saw everything he'd be leaving behind, would he be able to hold it together in front of her? By now she'd heard his hesitation, and he needed to say something.

"Yes. When?"

"Now. Please."

He'd been hiding behind a contract, but now that he'd heard her voice again, he knew something much deeper had been the real reason he'd been avoiding her and their baby. He was torn between his longing for freedom and allowing himself to love her…and start a family all over again. Some misguided loyalty to his daughters still held him back.

Funny how a man can convince himself he's a great guy, a fantastic father, live a decent life, be a fine doctor who cares about his patients, give to all the right charities, yet still be a coward—a coward who longs for freedom, whatever the hell that is, but who would never find happiness even if he stumbled through freedom's door. Not under these circumstances. Not since knowing René.

If he could make it through this visit and hold his ground, he'd be free to go back to the life he'd planned. Regardless of how empty it would be.

Jon arrived at René's house with armor firmly in place. He couldn't let her mesmerizing eyes lure him into changing his plans. He'd earned his freedom, damn it, and their contract spelled everything out. At least he hadn't let her down in that regard. If she expected more, well, that was her mistake. Not his.

One glance at her standing in the doorway with her hair full and resting on her shoulders, wearing oatmeal-colored pants and an olive-green tank top, and he forgot his house-of-straw plan.

René's heart had been bouncing around her rib cage since she'd called Jon, almost making her dizzy. Seeing him walk across her driveway toward her house sent a thousand flapping wings through her chest. She clutched the door frame for support, praying she'd recover before he came inside.

She couldn't help but stare at him. He wore his usual Saturday morning warm-up suit and running shoes, and he looked pale, maybe a little thinner than she'd remembered. He delved into her eyes with a questioning stare.

How should she begin?

She'd take the perfect hostess route, then work her way around to the heart of the matter—her *heart* and whether or not she *mattered* at all to him.

She forced a smile and held open the door for Jon. As if strangers, she wasn't sure how to greet him. A kiss on the cheek? A friendly hug? A mere handshake?

He saved her from making the decision by saying hello and giving her a quick, lackluster squeeze on the arm when he entered her house. The kernel of hope she'd sheltered and groomed in his absence withered a bit.

"You look good," he said, far too casually, his eyes betraying him.

"Thank you."

His gaze wandered around the room, as if looking for evidence of her son.

"Wow, I guess I should have sent a plant like everyone else," he said, looking a bit chagrined.

It tortured her for him to act like such a stranger.

"Evan's sleeping. Would you like to see him?"

He avoided her eyes, but nodded yes. If he didn't react to her son, she'd know for sure that he didn't care a damn about either of them.

"Of course," he said.

He followed her quietly down the hall to the

scene of their crime, her bedroom, where she'd set up the bassinet. When she opened the door and he could see the boy's head, he inhaled. A smile stretched across his lips and he leaned over the white wicker, the bassinet he'd helped her pick out and set up for her, to study the baby up close.

"Wow," he whispered.

After several seconds that seemed more like an eternity for someone holding her breath, he glanced at her.

"He's beautiful, René." The tender eyes she'd grown used to had returned.

Chills skimmed her skin. Their baby was living proof they should be together, but unless she told him how she felt, he would stick to the rule of contract.

"He looks like you. Don't you think?" she said.

He narrowed his eyes and pulled in his chin, then with a tilted head took another look at his son. She watched his forehead smooth, and his eyes soften. Slowly, like the sun peeking over the horizon, his smile returned.

He nodded. "He does, but I have a better hairline."

A laugh bubbled up her chest, the first in two weeks. The baby squirmed, and Jon put a finger over his lips.

They tiptoed out of her bedroom. Once safely back in the living room she sat on the sofa since her knees felt like noodles. The thought of baring her soul made her hands tremble.

He sat across from her, studying her every move. How would she get this out without collapsing? This might be her only chance to tell him, and she wasn't about to waste it.

"I think you should know I haven't been completely honest with you," she said.

He sat beside her with hands on his knees, eyes alert.

"Jon." Her voice quavered and she closed her eyes. "I love you."

He took a deep breath. "René." If he had anything else to say, it had stalled. His fingers found her hand and stroked it. "René."

This wasn't the response she'd hoped for, far from the bear hugs he was so good at giving, but she wouldn't give up. "I think I started loving you the day you said you'd be my birth coach, and when we made love, I knew for sure."

"But you never even hinted at it."

"I'd asked enough of you, and we had a contract."

"And I talked nonstop about leaving for China."

"And China," she repeated.

She sensed panic in his voice. Maybe it was a mistake, but at least now she knew for sure that he didn't feel the same way about her. That he was counting the moments before he could escape. She'd never have to guess again.

She pressed her lips together, to fight off the threatening tears. "Don't worry." She glanced at his restless eyes. "The contract stands. I just thought, that is, I hoped, that maybe…"

He shot up. "Love and commitment weren't part of the deal. Remember?"

"I wrote the rules. Yes. I remember." Her ribs clutched so hard she could hardly breathe. She didn't dare try to stand. He knelt in front of her and grasped her shoulders, his dark eyes piercing through her.

"René, honey, I can't do this. I can't start over. It's not that I don't care for you. I do. You have no idea. But I never would have consented to your deal if I thought it would turn out like this."

She hung her head, unable to bear looking at his reddening face and pleading eyes. She'd known the truth and insisted on trying to change it; how foolish of her to think three little words could make everything different. "Do you think I wanted this?"

He shook his head. "It took us both by surprise."

"I know," she mumbled.

Dead silence sucked the life out of the room.

"I've got to think things over," he said, grazing fingers over his hair. He skimmed her cheek with a kiss, gave her a lightning-quick hug, then dashed out her door.

A moment later she realized he hadn't even bothered to get in his car, but had taken off on foot.

Panic tore into Jon. The pavement burned through his running shoes. When he'd taken up long-distance running after his messy divorce, little did he know how handy it would come in.

So that's what he'd turned into, a man who ran from a woman who loved him and the inevitable commitment. An SOB who didn't plan to stick around for his son. Could a paltry journal make up for a missing father?

He scraped fingers over his head and increased the speed. He needed to burn, to sear, the guilt puncturing his resolve. Lacy would graduate next June. He'd leave for China the next week… except he still hadn't officially signed up for the trip and the deadline was quickly approaching.

Each tangy sea breath stung through his chest as he reached the shore. High tide. The waves lapped the sand in dependable rhythm, their fluorescent froth lingering as if to remind him what he'd left behind. A part of himself.

Come on, this wasn't in the plan. A beautiful woman asked him to donate some sperm and he'd agreed. How the hell shallow was he?

He glanced ahead. What were these people doing on the bike and jogging path? Couldn't they read the signs? A young couple pushed a stroller and moved to the side when he said, "On your left," as he passed. They smiled and waved at him, as if they were oblivious and happy.

Across the park lawn another couple, older compared to the first, pushed a double-wide stroller with twins, and the father shouldered a third child in some sort of backpack seat contraption. Why were they smiling?

The dark-haired woman's face morphed into René's. Ice invaded his chest and sent a chill down his spine. She'd be alone. Would she be smiling?

He thought of the devastated expression he'd left on her face just before he ran out her door.

He'd fallen in love with her, too. Damn it! He'd explained away every symptom over the past few months, and had convinced himself that the developing feelings were nothing more than midlife growing pains. A forty-two-year-old man gets propositioned—in an unconventional manner— by a gorgeous younger woman, and the giddy feelings that ensued were nothing more than flattery. That was the story he chose to stick to.

The easy conversations, the great meals, the stolen glances and secret thoughts had been figments of his imagination. His heightened sense of honor and duty to René were what any man in his situation would have done. The birth coaching? That was a bit overboard, but still, any other man in his place would have offered to do the same, wouldn't they? Did that equate love?

The constant thoughts about René had been another story. He'd conceded that he liked having her attention, her adulation, even if it had been a snow job to get what she wanted.

But that line of thinking never rang true about René, and he'd never allowed himself time to think things through in that regard. Besides, he knew firsthand she wasn't like that. And now, she'd told him she loved him.

Surely her profession of love was the product of postpartum blues and wonky hormones. When she came to her senses, she'd thank him for running off, leaving her to her original plan of single motherhood.

What was with the strollers today? He made a quick sidestep to avoid another one, an all-terrain stroller exactly like the one he'd given René. Just because it was a sunny October afternoon, did every family in Santa Barbara have to brandish their kids?

He made a U-turn and headed back on the grassy patch bordering the sidewalk. If he saw one more baby he'd yell.

I love you. René's words repeated in his brain. She'd bared her soul and what did he do? He ran away. Literally.

He let roll a string of curses blue enough to make a soldier blush, and prodded the running pace.

She'd looked so vulnerable sitting on her couch. Her eyes shone with emotion when she'd said she loved him, and instead of returning the sentiments, he'd tried to talk her out of it. He'd used the pitiful excuse of his sabbatical, his new job, his daughters and his divorce, then dropped her on her head and left.

He didn't deserve René.

She'd be better off without him. How could a woman like René—giving, fun, compassionate, tender, smart, sexy as all hell—consider him to be a person to love?

He tripped on a crack, flung forward and shoulder rolled back to his feet, as if he'd been kicked in the backside. He stood still while gathering his composure and looked around suspiciously. What the hell was that about?

As he started to run again, Evan's innocent face

appeared in his thoughts. He ran faster. How will he fare without a father in his life? A boulder of guilt landed in his stomach, rolling toward his toes, but it didn't slow his pace. How could he run away from them? What kind of man was he?

He saw yet another happy family out for a stroll. This time the young mother looked like Lacy. Hadn't she begged to babysit for René, then elbowed him, and with a knowing look and lift of her brow communicated how cool she thought René was? *I wish you could find someone like her.* Well, damn it, he had! Could his daughters accept a stepmother and half brother?

His ex-wife had pounded the point home that he wasn't good enough to spend a lifetime with. That's what René would want, a lifetime; what if he let her down, too? No, she'd be far better off without him.

Everyone would be better off if he stayed alone, yet he ran so fast he expected to spontaneously combust.

Who was he kidding?

He didn't want to be alone any more than he thought René wanted to be a single mother. And after two years it was more than time to kick Cherie and her negative comments to the curb. He was better than that. He deserved more. He deserved René. And Evan.

Here was this fantastic woman, the mother of his child, telling him she loved him, and he had a shot at a sweet kind of happiness he'd forgotten existed. He'd been so busy being a recluse, he'd put the possibility out of his mind. Thanks to his miserable divorce, he'd buried his feelings so deeply, he didn't even recognize the signs as they appeared one by one until he'd fallen in love with René.

Hell, he'd been in love with her for months. He just hadn't recognized it for what it was. It had happened in that moment when he couldn't let her go through the birthing classes alone. The moment he'd volunteered, he'd been hers. The same moment she'd said she'd fallen in love with him.

The contract stood in their way, and out of insecurity over his failed marriage, he'd let it. Used it, even.

Turns out, René loved him, too. That is, if she hadn't burned his picture in effigy since he ran out of her house—he glanced at his watch—a half hour ago. As if possible, he quickened his stride and thought his lungs might burst, but he deserved the pain. He'd hurt the woman he loved and he needed to get back to her before she changed her mind about him.

He needed to undo the hurt he'd caused. A jab of side-stitch pain felt like payback. He deserved several more, yet he smiled.

He loved her. Hell, yeah. He loved her, and couldn't wait to get to know his son!

The palm trees blurred past. His breath came in rhythmical spurts. Heading back to René's he'd never run with such purpose in his entire life.

René had come undone. She'd melted into a puddle of tears and cried until she thought she'd heave. It was all her fault. She'd been the one to come up with this idea of having a kid with no strings attached, but she hadn't bargained on Jon becoming everything she'd always wished for.

He'd been there for her: dependable, strong, funny at the most unpredictable moments, tender at others. He was a father through and through. The love for his daughters shimmered from his eyes whenever he spoke about them, which was often. It pained her to realize Evan would never know such love from his father. Could she make up for it? Would she be enough?

She'd tried to compose herself, washed her face, checked on her son who was still sleeping, fortunately, and made herself a cup of pepper-mint-and-chamomile tea. She needed something to help settle her stomach and calm her nerves before she next nursed Evan. It was so much harder to let down her milk when she was nervous or uptight.

Oddly, her crying jag had left her feeling a modicum of relief. If only it were permanent. Since sobbing, she'd attained a state of repose that felt a bit like levitating over hot coals, and she waited to fall into the fire as she sipped her tea.

Movement by the avocado tree caught her eye. It was Jon racing toward her porch. Her stomach took flight. She jumped up as he hammered on her door. She opened it and he blew in like the north wind, strong, brisk and with a biting scent.

Jon dug his fingers into her hair and angled her

face toward his, then planted a firm kiss on her mouth. Just as quickly he broke free.

"Forgive me. Please forgive me," he huffed.

He kissed her again, this time clutching her flush to his body. "I was such a jerk. No. I was a complete ass. How could I be so awful to you?" He nuzzled her neck and kissed her beneath her jaw. "Please don't hate me." Another kiss, this one on her brow. "I love you. God, I love you."

"Jon," she said, barely a sound.

"Tell me you forgive me. Please." He grazed her ear with another kiss, then whispered, "Please."

She hesitated. *You love me?* Could she forget the heartbreak he'd put her through for the past two weeks, and the devastation he'd left in his wake when he'd run off after she'd told him she loved him? Had she heard him right? He loved her?

If he thought he could break into her house, kiss her up and make everything all better, just like that, he had another think coming.

But she couldn't deny how her heart nearly burst when she saw him run back to her. Relief greater than anything she'd ever known had coursed through her veins at the mere sight of him. Her lips found his neck and tasted the salt from his sheen. Why had she kissed him if she hated him? If she couldn't forgive him?

He'd come back to her, knowing full well that she loved him, professing his love in return. What more proof did she need?

"I forgive you," she said, barely audible.

"You do? Fantastic."

He hugged her as if she might disappear if he let go.

"I want the world to know who Evan's father is," he said, waltzing her around the room. She was incapable of resisting. "I want to be there for him when he takes his first step, reads his first book, throws his first baseball, when he kisses his first girl. I want to see it all, watch him grow, hear his voice change, send him off to college and then… maybe you'll come with me to China?"

She laughed at his audacity.

"You do forgive me, don't you?"

His intense brown eyes blasted into hers; she could hardly stand to look at them. They made her knees get wobbly and her mind fog up. She was angry as blazes at him, remember? Forgiveness was one thing, but what about trust?

He cupped her arms and held her in place. "I want to love you every day for the rest of my life. I want you to be the first face I see in the morning and the body I hold to fall asleep."

"Jon." It sounded more like a plea.

"I love you, René, and I know you love me, too." He pulled back and smiled at her. "You already told me, remember?"

She cuffed his arm. "And you ran off."

"I promise never to run off again."

"What about that new job?"

"Leave the MidCoast Clinic? Never."

Could she believe him? He *had* come through on all of his other promises to her. You bet she could.

The nursery monitor crackled with mewing and grunts. Evan was waking up. She took Jon's hand and led him down the hall. Together they watched their boy stretch and curl until he found his voice and made a heartfelt cry.

She reached for him. Jon stopped her.

"Let me," he said.

When he held their son with noticeable confidence, René let free the breath she'd been holding. This wasn't a dream. This was Jon being the father she'd wished for.

Jon rocked Evan in the crook of his arm, and smiled at her. This time, she was the one to offer a kiss along with her heart, and he eagerly accepted both.

Her mother's saying repeated in her mind yet again—*be careful what you wish for.*

How true. René had wished for a baby of her own, but it turned out she hadn't wished big enough. Things hadn't turned out as she'd planned—they'd ended up even better.

Her yearning for a family had been short by one person—a father. The desire had been so buried she hadn't even known it. Now, with Jon at her side holding her son, *their* son, a grander and more perfect wish had finally been granted.

EPILOGUE

One month later

"HURRY, Jon, or we'll be late," René said, slipping on her second earring.

Jon kissed Evan one last time before handing him over to Lacy. She grinned and cuddled her half brother as if her own.

"Don't worry about a thing," she said. "I've got both of your cell numbers, Claire is just a few blocks away and I'm getting really good at taking care of my brother." She kissed the boy. "Wait until Amanda finds out. She'll be so jealous."

It would be their first night out together since the baby had been born and he'd moved in. Just the two of them having dinner in a special seaside restaurant without a single interruption. Heaven.

His daughter gave him a kiss on the cheek

followed by a knowing look. He planned to pro-
pose to René tonight and Lacy couldn't disguise
her suspicions. They'd marry in the summer,
when Amanda had a break from her studies and
could attend.

He'd start his sabbatical this summer, too, but
China was the last thing on his mind. Nope. He'd
decided to take the year off, anyway—to be a
house husband while René continued her practice.
He thought of it as a grand adventure, something
only a guy full of surprises might do, an adventure he wouldn't miss for the world. And René
practically jumped with glee when he'd told her
his astounding plan.

He stood grinning like an idiot at his daughter
and son.

René's long slender fingers circled his wrist.
"Are you ready?" she asked.

"You bet I am." He glanced at her empty ring
finger, then patted the small box in his jacket
pocket. That finger wouldn't be empty much
longer.

MEDICAL™

Large Print

Titles for the next three months...

March

DATING THE MILLIONAIRE DOCTOR	Marion Lennox
ALESSANDRO AND THE CHEERY NANNY	Amy Andrews
VALENTINO'S PREGNANCY BOMBSHELL	Amy Andrews
A KNIGHT FOR NURSE HART	Laura Iding
A NURSE TO TAME THE PLAYBOY	Maggie Kingsley
VILLAGE MIDWIFE, BLUSHING BRIDE	Gill Sanderson

April

BACHELOR OF THE BABY WARD	Meredith Webber
FAIRYTALE ON THE CHILDREN'S WARD	Meredith Webber
PLAYBOY UNDER THE MISTLETOE	Joanna Neil
OFFICER, SURGEON...GENTLEMAN!	Janice Lynn
MIDWIFE IN THE FAMILY WAY	Fiona McArthur
THEIR MARRIAGE MIRACLE	Sue MacKay

May

DR ZINETTI'S SNOWKISSED BRIDE	Sarah Morgan
THE CHRISTMAS BABY BUMP	Lynne Marshall
CHRISTMAS IN BLUEBELL COVE	Abigail Gordon
THE VILLAGE NURSE'S HAPPY-EVER-AFTER	Abigail Gordon
THE MOST MAGICAL GIFT OF ALL	Fiona Lowe
CHRISTMAS MIRACLE: A FAMILY	Dianne Drake

Z545929